REBORN

Book One of

RISE OF THE REALMS

D. FISCHER

Reborn (Rise of the Realms: Book One)

Copyright © 2018 by D. Fischer

ASIN: B07839PHJ5

ISBN-13: 978-1981943524 (CreateSpace-Assigned)
ISBN-10: 1981943528
BISAC: Fiction / Fantasy / Epic

I'd love to just take a moment and thank all the 'underdogs' out there who have to fight for what they want. Strength comes within - it starts with you - and just because you have to work harder for it, doesn't mean you're not meant to have it.

Fight for what's yours and don't let anyone stand in your way.

Dream big. You lack nothing.

Everything in this book is fictional. It is not based on true events, persons, or creatures that go bump in the night, no matter how much we wish it were...

CONTENTS

PROLOGUE

KATRIANE DUPONT

EARTH REALM

THE PAST

The frigid winter air seeps into my bones, freezing them down to the marrow. The skin on my cheeks resists it, shriveling and burning with each subtle, chilly breeze. Even with the layers I wear—the coat, a long sleeve shirt, hat, and mittens—I might as well be wearing nothing at all.

I shiver as I glance around, my muscles quaking against the cloth; its only job is to keep me warm. Absentmindedly, my numb, mitten-covered fingers twirl the ladle, sloshing the contents inside my simmering pot as my head swivels at every subtle noise within the forest. My paranoia has the better of me. The closer I get to finishing my potion, the more my mind concocts its own brew of fear-laced emotions.

I glance back at my boiling pot. As each bubble reaches the surface, a few stray drops splatter into the air and splash against the side of the cast-iron cauldron. The fire licks up its sides, desperately trying to consume the cauldron itself, considering it a challenge. The snow melts around my makeshift fire pit, creating a cold puddle at my feet. The frigid liquid seeps through my tennis shoes and soaks my socks. As the bubbles rise from the bottom and free themselves once they hit the top, the crackling noise of the flames and the popping of each bubble echo in the quiet winter night. The full moon is the only thing that lights my vision aside from the fire, a beacon aiding me in my quest in this thick blanket of trees.

I'm about to do something forbidden, something I know I shouldn't. This could be my demise, my destruction. The chilly air isn't the only thing that makes my muscles quiver, knocking my knees together. I could be punished and cease to exist. I'm aware of the consequences my actions could, or will, have.

I take a deep breath, fog leaving my nostrils on the exhale, and let go of the handle. The wooden ladle clinks against the cast iron as I bend to the ground and reach inside my brown, leather satchel. I was given this satchel during my Right, the ceremony that brought me into my rightful place as a witch.

My mother gave it to me during the celebration following that ceremony. Such a look of joy had crossed her face as I unwrapped it from its box. It was perfect, smooth; I had run my fingers along the pristinely knit hems and the embedded half-moon circle with a line down the middle—my coven's crescent.

But now, the edges fray, and stains from previous potions mar the once smooth, leather surface; and a tear is beginning to form in the middle of the strap. I refuse to be rid of it, though. This is the gift that was given to me, my first gift as a rightful witch. It's the symbol of my place among this world, no longer the girl I used to be but of the witch I must become.

I flip open the flap and grip my hand around the last ingredient. The bottle is smooth and slick against my mitten-covered fingers. Standing up straight, I close my eyes, taking another deep breath while trying to cease my quaking. *This is it. No turning back.*

My phone buzzes inside my fluffy, winter coat, and I jump at the abrupt noise, almost dropping the vial. The breath leaves my lungs in a rush, flooding me with relief, grateful for the distraction before a concerned frown pinches my eyebrows together.

It's after midnight. Who would call me at this hour?

Fishing it from my pocket, I see my mother's name appear on my screen. My phone chirps at me, pleading with me to answer the video chat. Hesitating for just a moment, I swipe the screen to accept the call, and my mother's moving face comes onto the screen, along with the white sheets of the bed she lay beneath.

I suck in a breath, the sight of her not for the faint of heart. My chest aches, seeing her in such a condition.

Her face is sunken in, her chocolate-colored eyes hollow inside their sockets. Those eyes used to be filled with such warmth but now are stained with blood, shedding tears as they plead with me. She coughs before she can mutter her greeting. "Katriane, don't do it."

I feign innocence, though my voice shakes, giving away my lie before I have time to voice the entire sentence. "I don't know what you're talking about."

Her sunken eyes narrow, the skin pulling too tight around their lids. Her once slightly aged and wrinkled skin now appears paper thin. "I've seen what you're about to do, Katriane. You mustn't . . . it's forbidden."

I sigh loudly and glance around, avoiding those eyes that will haunt me for the rest of my life if I don't follow through with my plan. I don't look for anything in particular, but I can't keep looking at my mother and the reminder that the fated weight of the witches now resting upon my shoulders. Watching the blood dribble down a mother's cheek to her jawbone would break any child's heart. I'll do anything to make it stop.

My mother, Janine, is the psychic of our coven. I should have known she'd see what I'm about to do. This wasn't exactly a planned mission, but deep down in my bones, I knew it was necessary. Forbidden or not.

Demi-Lune, my coven, is suffering at the hands of an incurable illness. We've just learned that this illness is taking out witches from every coven. We don't know where it comes from, how we got it, or how to cure it. We only know that it brings the blackest of deaths. The virus—or whatever it is—is eating the host's body from the inside out. The vital organs inside the infected bodies are bleeding, sucking the blood from their necessary veins like the vampires that plague Earth. We've tried everything—a trusted, real human doctor, potions, pleading with Erline—but nothing has worked.

My mother barks out another cough, and my attention zones back to the tiny screen. I watch as she pulls the napkin from her mouth. Blood soaks the soft tissue before it leaves the sight of the camera.

"You cannot summon Erline. Dealing with Mother Nature—the Fee—always comes with a price."

Erline is the Fee in charge of this realm—of Earth's realm. Many call her Mother Nature and believe her to be a mythical creature, needing a face and name to blame the one who causes mayhem and destruction. But she's real—a Fee, or Faery as some may call them. There are many Fee, each controlling their own realm like it's their godly right. But my only plea is for the one who controls this realm . . . the one who made us and the one who should hold some measure of mercy for her daughters.

I lower my voice just above a mumble. "I know they do, but someone has to do it, or you'll die. The coven, the witches—they'll all die."

She shakes her head, her unwashed, greasy hair unmoving. "Don't you think Erline knows that? She would have done something by now if she were capable." She pauses. "Katriane, if you summon her, it'll have severe consequences."

"There is no choice," I scream into the phone, impatient, my nerves raw and exposed. Time is running out. I don't have time to argue with logic when logic has failed us.

She remains quiet, shocked by my outburst. "This action will bring about an untrustworthy beast and confuse the realms," she whispers, attempting once more to talk me out of it. "If you do this . . . if you follow through . . . I've seen what that beast can do. It'll bring about the reincarnate of the First Born, Katriane. Our lives are not worth that kind of risk."

I suck in a shaky breath, her words frightening me like she knew they would. Erline created all in this realm—the beasts, the land, the people. She also created her first child with the help of Kheelan, the Fee in charge of the Death Realm. Together, a daughter was created. The First Born witch, Myla.

Erline, fearful that Kheelan would be her daughter's demise, hid Myla from him. But Erline's protectiveness and sense of possession—that of which only a mother would feel—was what brought Myla's death in the end, or so the stories say. It is said she sacrificed herself. For what, I'm not sure.

"If you do this, if you follow through, all could be lost. The future would remain uncertain. Even I cannot see what is foretold."

"You don't know that," I mumble.

She stares at me, searching my eyes through the screen. Her jaw ticks, more prominent with the lack of muscle and fat surrounding her protruding bones.

My mother lowers her voice. "You need to let this illness run its course. If we lose some of our coven . . ."

"I don't accept that," I snap, my eyes narrowing. "This virus is designed only for death."

My mother pleads with me before I press the red end key, ending the video chat. Her face now gone from my screen, the noiseless woods cause a shiver to run up my spine. There's no sign of life out here, no noise for distractions or comfort.

I pocket my phone and hold the vial of herbs in front of me. Taking a deep breath, I uncork it and gently tap a few flakes into the boiling water. I watch the pot, and for a few moments, nothing happens. Relief mixed with frustration settles in the pit of my stomach.

Just as I release a flustered sigh, the ground shakes. At first, it's a quiet little rumble off in the distance, but as it grows nearer, the drifts of snow shake. The flakes bounce against each other and level their piles by the waves.

My cauldron's contents slosh, but I don't dare grab it. I step back, narrowly avoiding the hot liquid as the cauldron tips over. It melts the snow in its wake and rivers down the slope, the fire diminishing and casting darkness all around me.

I glance around, turning full circle, until the wind picks up. The snowflakes sail in every direction, whipping me in the face and freezing my skin. I do my best to shield my face, regretting the choice I made by summoning our Mother.

Chanting a spell in the tongue of my ancestral magic, my lips move at a rapid speed. In my desperate state, the words are louder than they need to be as I try to create a shield using my own wind to keep the stinging snow at bay.

The spell takes effect, the freezing pain no longer rubbing my skin raw, and I blink my eyes. Several tears fall down the humps of my burning cheeks, and I watch the snow take a different route once it connects with my own winds.

Luckily, my black hair is short and isn't affected much from this unnatural occurrence. The burn on my raw skin from my tears is a painful reminder of my mother's condition . . . a reminder of why I'm here, why I'm doing this.

I glance around, the blizzard making it difficult to see anywhere but a few feet in front of me. Twigs and leaves from the fall season begin to mix with the snow, beating against every tree, every surface it runs into.

The wind stops, so sudden that my heart skips a beat. I chant the words to drop my own spell, the cold winter air feeling warmer now that it isn't being whipped around at subfreezing temperatures.

Flakes of snow and debris fall dead to the ground as if they were never disturbed to begin with. The footsteps from my entrance are gone, making the scene look like it's freshly fallen. It's so quiet I can hear my own breaths escape my lips, and my heart pounds inside my chest, causing the vein in my neck to throb.

The air shimmers and waves in front of me. I hold my breath. A form takes shape; colors swirl and churn, invading certain sections of the shimmering figure until a full body stands before me. I release the air from my lungs, a puff of mist slithering from my mouth, and I'm left speechless.

Erline is beautiful. Long, blond hair reaches the back of her knees. A light dress, the color of her pale skin, drops to the snow-covered ground, matching its surface as it drapes past her ankles and out behind her. The skirt of the dress resembles a river, flowing as if it cascades around a bend.

I move my eyes to her face as she tilts her head up from looking at the ground. The most angelic features cause me to hitch a breath. Straight, medium-sized nose, perfect cheekbones, flush, rosy patches in all the right areas. She'd be striking if it wasn't for her black, unnatural eyes. No whites, no colors, no irises—just black orbs inserted where normal eyes should be.

She opens her plush, red lips, a slight sneer lifting the curve of her nostrils. "My daughters do not summon me," she growls. Her voice, though thick with condescension, is like beautiful wind chimes orchestrating a song I've never heard.

Her black eyes, her voice, her presence, hypnotizes me and I give a little shake to my head. "I had no choice," I mumble once I find my voice. It sounds meek even to my own ears.

"There is always a choice!" she yells, her beautiful features twisting in such malicious anger.

I take a step back, frightened. "Erline . . . I— I need your help."

Her eyes narrow. "I know all about the death disease, my daughter. What makes you think you have the right to ask me for a cure?"

I double blink. If she knew all about it, why hasn't she helped us? Why does she allow it to continue? "The disease will wipe the covens from existence. I thought . . ." I frown and stand up straighter, finding my backbone and steeling my heart, "I thought of all people—beings, whatever—that you'd rather we existed than not. We're your flesh and blood."

Her eyes continue to smother me as her jaw ticks with her obvious annoyance. I threw her words back in her face. We're her daughters, not her creations. She should be helping us. I'm beginning to hold little faith for this woman, this Fee who stands before me.

Erline's curled lip lowers, smoothing back to that luminescent and youthful-looking skin as she reaches some sort of conclusion. "And you're willing to pay the price?" her voice sings.

Relief fills my heart, chasing away the sense of dread. However, I chew the inside of my lip, the taste of blood hitting my tongue, and I consider the possibilities of what this *price* might be. Making deals with the Fee always comes with its own set of consequences. My heart jumps, skipping beats as my fear skyrockets. *Here goes nothing.* "Yes."

A toothy, sweet smile lifts her lips at the corners. Her perfect teeth seem to glow as she takes a graceful step closer. "So be it."

Without further questions being voiced on my part, she raises a delicate hand. The snow, the dead, sticky, wet leaves, and twigs swirl around me. My body becomes weightless, my feet leaving the ground as I'm lifted from it. I panic, feet kicking in the empty air. I want to scream, but the oxygen leaves my lungs in a desperate attempt to escape. White light seeps from my pores, illuminating the night around me and blinding my eyes. My skin feels hot, too hot, as I fight for breath. Each vein smolders, and every pore burns. Pain, unlike any I've ever felt, begins in my bones and curls my toes. They crack, reshape, reform. I clutch my hand around my neck as it turns into a claw with pointed talons, trying to fight for much-needed air. Pain blossoms in my head—a dull ache at first before a thousand invisible knives sear through my temples, blooming like a flower.

The wind stops, and I drop to the ground. Landing on my feet—or what were once my feet—my lungs fill with blessed oxygen. My chest expands beyond the limit I'm used to, and the sound that leaves my nostrils as I exhale is far too loud, like a horse after a lengthy race.

I lift my head and glance around. Everything is brighter, sharper, even in the pitch-black night. Every detail, every bending line, curve, and spike of each snowflake is detectible as my vision adjusts.

Involuntarily, my eyes flit to Erline. The smile on her face has grown into a genuine one, filled with love and adoration. I stare at her skin, my new vision making it possible to see the smaller details. Pores—she has no pores.

Her lips whisper, "Darling?"

As if they're not my own eyes, they lift to hers. When I try to speak, my lips don't move. Frustrated, I try again, and nothing happens.

What did you do to me? I shout in my head. At the non-verbal yell, a puff of smoke curls from my nose, and a feeling of irritation that's different from my own can be felt. In my peripheral vision, I see a black snout, scaled but sleek.

"No need to shout, Katriane. I can hear you just fine." She smiles, tilting her head to the side.

I attempt to double blink though my eyelids don't move. I feel like I'm watching her like a child sitting in front of a TV. My body shifts, and my head lowers, except it's not my head . . . or my body.

"Darling," she coos again, reaching out a hand to place a gentle stroke on my skin. But it's not my skin. I can feel it, but I know it's not mine. "Welcome back."

I frown, but my eyebrows don't move. *What's going on*, I ask quietly, a little frightened to know the answer.

"This is your cure." Erline laughs. "The price you must pay—to share a body with another."

She holds out a hand, and a shape swirls inside her unlined palm before a vial appears. "Go ahead, darling," she says to me. I get the feeling she's not talking to me this time. After all, I have no idea what she wants.

Erline's eyes roam my form, her words just above a mumble, "I can't bring back my daughter's body, but I can bring back her spirit in her second form. A form of fire and scales, reborn to this world."

I feel my eyes get wetter, beads of dew saturate the rims of my eyelids, and a few tears drop from their corners. She holds the vial to my cheek, catching the droplets.

Corking the bottle, she holds it up to her eyes and says, "This is your cure. A drop of the First Born's tears will cure the incurable." She glances past the bottle and back into my eyes, hesitating for a moment. "This is not my disease, not of my creation, Katriane. Your blame is misplaced. Now that a price is paid, this wrong can be righted."

I feel my chest expand for several seconds before the loudest roar leaves my lips, shaking the trees, disrupting the soundless night. A call of freedom, I realize.

What have I done?

CHAPTER ONE

DYSON COLEMAN

DEATH REALM

Rubbing my temples, I attempt to ease the headache forming behind them and threatening to take over. I didn't know a shade could even get a headache until now. *For the love of—make it stop.*

The shouting in the room raises another level. I drop my transparent hands and glance around at those gathered before me. Time . . . we need time. Time is short to come by, even for the dead.

I glance at my feet, leaning my weightlessness against my heels, desperately trying to tune out the noise of chattering, angry shades. It's still so new to me, not having any weight to shift, just to ease the tension of a muscle. Reaper's Breath floats just above the ground, twirling and swaying around my legs like an annoying pet begging for a scratch behind the ears.

Kheelan, Fee ruler of the Death Realm, created the Reaper's Breath as his pet, so to speak. Its disloyalty to its owner has yet to be discovered by the owner. I'm not naïve enough to believe Kheelan will never discover the disloyalty of his subjects—of the rebellion. Deceit comes back to haunt, no matter the cause or how carefully planned. It's only a matter of time before the asshole discovers us and our plan, hence the shortage of time.

Since I arrived here, Reaper's Breath has been obsessed with me. A tendril of its swirling fog follows me almost everywhere I go. It's like the stray dog I never asked for.

Threats start erupting, and I take a deep breath before shouting, "Shut up!" Though I usually have a lot of patience, my nerves are raw, my head is pounding, and these ignorant friends of mine can't seem to get along for five seconds so we can come up with a logical fucking plan.

It takes a minute for the voices to die down, but eventually, they do. I breathe a sigh of relief; some of my raw emotions leave my body as the air rushes from my lungs. The breath is unnecessary—the dead don't need to breathe. But old habits die hard.

A dozen sets of eyes swivel in my direction, their bodies mushed against the stone walls inside my small assigned room. Since we are all transparent, I can meet each set of eyes, no matter who they stand behind. It used to be unnerving, but I've found it can be useful.

I place my feet flat against the stone floor and cross my arms. "Look, I know you're concerned about the shift. No one has answers as to why I was able to cross over, but I did. There's no point in yelling at each other's theories."

In truth, I knew more than they did, but I can't trust everyone with my secret. I plan to keep these lips shut, at least for the time being. Kheelan's loyalty is gained by cruelty. Many flock to him with secrets just so they can remain safely tucked under his little Fee armpit.

When I first arrived here, Reaper's Breath aided me in visiting my Pack mate, Flint. I was a wolf-shifter . . . *am* a wolf-shifter . . . with unfinished business. The haunting happened to be during a battle in revenge for my death, but I still gave my last wordless goodbye.

I don't know what Reaper's Breath sees in me; maybe it took sympathy on me when Kheelan bound my wolf inside me, but it's the most loyal creature I've found since I died. And though I'm dead, I'm still a wolf-shifter, but a wolf-shifter whose wolf is no longer allowed its freedom can break the man and the beast inside.

Either way, I'm grateful for Reaper's Breath's help for giving me a shred of hope. But the help I'll ask from it in the future will definitely be extensive. I briefly close my eyes, hoping like hell it won't abandon me now.

I continue, scratching the back of my neck. "The only point is, how are we going to take advantage of this opportunity? Of this shift in realms?"

"You're talking about a rebellion, Dyson," Chad says, skepticism thick in his voice as his eyes narrow. He's not the only skeptic in the room. Through him, I can see the others behind him, their lips zipped shut in a fine line as they keep their words of agreement at bay. "How are shades going to rebel against a Fee? We wouldn't get past his vampire army, let alone settle a finger on Kheelan himself."

Vampires could be a complication. They're also Kheelan's creation. Rumor has it that he created them a long time ago to search for his long-lost daughter. Since then, they've turned less "investigators" and more "bloodthirsty beasts." You can't control a beast that is fueled by actual life and the blood that pumps through their veins. A vampire's loyalty will always remain with its next meal.

My lips form a thin line, and my upper body angles forward. "What do vampires need to survive?"

Jane's slightly wrinkled forehead furrows as her fingers adjust her pink floral nightgown before she pipes up, "Blood."

I allow a small half-smile. "Exactly. Shades don't have blood."

Chad's eyebrows raise, sarcasm thick in his voice to the point where I want to reach out and smack him across his ignorant face. "They have their own means of torture for us,

Dyson. You know that." He huffs and looks away. "A ghost versus a vampire . . . I wonder who will win."

****

The shades start to leave my room, floating through the wall one at a time, per my instruction. It wouldn't do to draw attention to ourselves and our gathered meeting that literally got us nowhere.

Jane stands next to a petite woman I don't recognize, a warm smile on her face. I quirk an eyebrow at Jane before settling my eyes back on the woman's small face. Her nose is small, the bridge of it short. Freckles sprinkle across her cheeks, and her lips are large and full against her face.

"Yes?" I ask.

Jane swings out an arm toward the woman. "This is Tanya. Can we—" Jane glances around. "Can we talk?"

I clear my throat unnecessarily and unfold my arms from across my chest. "Sure."

"I need a favor," Tanya asks, opening her mouth and spilling the words before Jane has the chance.

Dipping my chin, I eye her from under my lashes. Her abrupt exclamation grates against my already raw nerves. I can't straddle another ego right now. "I'm not in any position to give out favors."

Jane's face pinches, a slight glint of anger in her eyes. "You have Reaper's Breath's attention, Dyson. You and I both know that creature was what helped you. Hear her out."

Tanya twists her fingers, their joints bending to accommodate the assault she forces upon them. Her sudden anxiety twists at my non-beating heart. "My son . . ." she begins.

TEMBER

THE PRESENT

Perched on the edge of the brick building, I watch my charge, Katriane Dupont, walk into her shop. My drenched, long curls whip about my face with the force of the wind rolling up the side of the brick below me. My dress clings to my skin, and my white, feathered wings rustle against my back in agitation, cascading droplets of rain. Her footsteps are light but careful, her grace becoming legendary amongst the Guardian Realm.

A witch expelled from her coven is a vulnerable one, and for a reason I can't fathom, the creatures of the dead flock to her like Earth Realm bugs to a light.

It's late. The stars should twinkle in the night sky, but the roaring storm consumes them with its thunderous veracity. This is a wet fall the Earth Realm is having, a sure sign that its winter will be a strong and vicious one.

The bell chimes as she opens the glass door to her shop, echoing against the buildings of the empty street. Soon she disappears from my view, confined to the safety of her home. I watch as the lights flick on in the second story of the building, and my heart eases. She's safe. My job is half-way done, but the questions forming in my head have yet to be answered.

My eyes return to the danger threatening my charge's safety. In the alley, just beside her shop, two pairs of red eyes lurk like roaches, concealed by the dark shadows as they hunch close to the ground. They wait for the moment of visible weakness to strike my unsuspecting Katriane, but unfortunately for them, they'll never have the chance.

Slowly, I stand from my perched position and expand my wings before flexing the muscles in my back, beating them against the air. The sound is drowned by the thunder, and my body lifts into the night. Taking the higher route so as to not be seen, I fly the short distance to Katriane's building and perch once more. As a hundreds of years old angel, my movements are fluid and quiet with practiced ease. The enemies on the ground, none-the-wiser, have little knowledge I watch them like a hawk stalking its next feast. Over my dead, immortal body will any vampire lay a claw or fang on my charge.

They begin speaking to each other, but all I hear is the slight hissing at the end of each word, their lips attempting to make coherent sounds around their permanently elongated fangs. I curse Kheelan for the day he created these monstrosities. They're assassins, their only purpose to do Kheelan's bidding. They're a plague to the world, a disgrace to the realms and that of the Fee who had created them so long ago. There was a time that these creatures of the dead didn't exist, and each realm was all the better for it.

Thick, oiling revulsion rolls in the pit of my stomach. Only a sick mind could create such a monster, such a contradiction to life itself, and then unleash them on this innocent realm. My fingers grip the edge of the wall between my feet, my knuckles straining against my skin as I fight my inner hatred.

Silently, they make their way to the edge of the alley. No longer worried about their concealment, they walk through the middle instead of skimming, crouched, along the wall. I sigh at their ignorance and spread my wings once more, leaping from the edge and dropping to the ground in a dive.

It's a short fall, but as my feet touch the wet cement with a grace few creatures possess, the vampires' sensitive hearing picks up the extra step as I take it.

They whip their heads around, their red eyes deep like pools of blood puddled on the floor. I imagine those eyes themselves would strike fear into any victim.

Veins, black as the night sky, are visible through their pale skin, and fangs dip past their bottom lips, poking the skin just above their chins. The smell of rotting, dead flesh wrinkles my nose, and my stomach rolls once more.

"Evening boys," I greet with much more kindness than they deserve. I tilt my head. "Care to share your plans for this fine night?"

They step from the shadows, and I get a better view of their profiles. One has red hair and a pinched nose; the other has black hair, matching the veins inside his skin. Both tall and broad, I imagine Kheelan sent them for their intimidating size alone.

The red-haired vampire hisses at me, red-tinged spittle flying from his mouth. The rain, flattening his hair to his forehead, causes him to look more like a vulnerable living being, but he's not. No vampire is a living being, and each should be judged accordingly for their crimes—I'd be honored to deliver the verdict.

Quicker than the rain that pounds the ground and the lightning that strikes the land, they race toward me. But I'm prepared. I bend my knees, ducking and spreading my wings. As I spin on the balls of my bare feet, my wings hit the vampires against their torsos, sending them crashing into the brick wall. Before they can fall to the ground, I rush forward, reach out my hands, and capture their necks. Their skin feels slick—like the carcass of a plucked chicken—but not from the downpour. The feel of the skin against mine threatens the hold of my fingers, their grips, and the contents within my stomach.

Pinned to the man-made rock, their fingers claw my hands, but it's useless—I don't feel it. Angels are built to be indestructible to any enemy of the night—we have far more strength than any vampire.

"Do you think the Death Realm has a place for the twice dead?" I whisper to them, my face relaxed as I easily hold them prisoner. They hiss, and guttural growls pass chomping teeth. I blink, unaffected, and twist my hands to the side. The snap of their spines rings true, announcing my easy victory. Within another blink, they're piles of dust pooled against the concrete. I watch as rain flows along the grooves, mixing with their ashes and carrying them away to the street drain just beyond.

"I suppose they'll find out," I mumble to myself.

Glancing down the alleyway, both left and right, I make sure that's the last of them before soaring back into the sky, the rain beating against my skin from my gathering speed.

****

The ocean ripples, and waves rumble below me. Its salty aroma piques my curiosity. Could it possibly taste as bitter as it smells?

My feet purposefully dip into the chilled water as I soar toward the gates of my realm. The ocean is angry this evening, pitch-black and heavy with towering walls of water before they roll and crash back into the main body.

My wings beat, fighting against the winds with such ease. I'm getting close; the gate should be just ahead. Adjusting my body, I angle my feathers. One–two– strong beats of their large expanse, and I'm soring to the clouds, my long hair whipping behind me.

Pouring rain soaks my body, my clothes, and when I pass through the black churning clouds, the electricity tickles my skin as a lightning bolt passing straight through me. It's thrilling, sending a prickling sense of delight through every inch of my veins, my nerves, and I smile, pushing harder until the storm clouds break. This is what freedom feels like.

Breathing a sigh of contentment, the grin still plastered on my face, I hover above the clouds. The feeling of power that comes from my own immortality has an unequal comparison. To be anything but what I am, and my existence would be incomplete.

What a different view it is from this side. The storm churns just the same as the water below. It rolls before dipping inside its expanse, like churning dough, while force feeding the Earth its tormenting rage. Lightning illuminates the clouds, creating a deep purple no other earthly color can match. They rumble with each strike of electricity, a threat to its oncoming and increasing assault.

I have much respect for the ocean. It's an environment all its own, constantly breaking the rules and crossing the line but respected just the same. The ocean and I are much alike.

Tilting my head away from the storm just below my feet, I take in the view of the sky and the details of the Milky Way. Each star seems to twinkle on its own against a black backdrop for its fine glory. What mysteries do they hold? Peace and calm above me, torture and rage below.

The Earth Realm is a beautiful one, but I imagine there's more out there. There's always more out there. Adventure is what I crave, what every angel craves. We're guardians, expected to keep watch over the realms and serve justice to those deserving. As adventurous as that sounds, it's often not enough to sate us. Like racehorses going for a light jog, we need the run of the track to calm our insatiable nerves.

My quick eyes spot a distraction—the shimmering gates to my realm, home. The Guardian Realm, run by Erma, the Fee who created us. To me, she is much more than my creator.

My smile fading, I flap my wings once more and soar toward the gates, which are almost invisible to the eye unless you're Fee born.

I arrive closer to the gate, my feathers touching the swirling tip. It sucks me in like a vortex. A human would never survive the passing. It rips me apart and puts me back together again, but I don't feel pain. I was born to not feel pain, to show no mercy or weakness, to be neither consumed nor struck paralyzed by cold or heat.

Once back together, it shoves me through, my bare feet landing on the black marble floor. The floor looks alive—the white specks dotted throughout move on their own like schools of fish inside a pond.

Black night sky hangs overhead, the stars much brighter here, closer than they are to the Earth Realm, dimly lighting the place I call home. I can no longer hear the ocean, the rumble of clouds from the Earth Realm, and a small part of me wants to turn back, to go watch if but for a moment longer. The Guardian Realm doesn't exist inside Earth's. There are no oceans here. Just like all the other realms, we each belong to our own plain equivalent to Earth's.

My white-feathered wings come into my peripheral view before folding against my back like a tight embrace. I step forward, nodding to a few fellow angels—men and women— gathered near the entrance. I keep my eyes on them as they go back to chatting in hushed tones, gossip surely the topic flicking off their tongues.

Angels may be guardians, but that doesn't exempt them from evil doing. Angels are not always . . . angels. Many slack, ignoring their charges and duties. Some even tip the scale to the dark side, enduring that extra thrill we crave to such extreme measures. I suppose with light, there must always be a dark.

"Tember," a warm, familiar voice coos my name.

My head swivels around, my wet, brown curls slapping against my cheek before my eyes gaze upon my Fee creator. Her shoulder-length, cropped, red hair flows in a non-existent breeze as she advances to me with open arms. She's strikingly beautiful as all Fee tend to be. She's short, about my height of

5'2'' in Earth Realm measurement. Her eyes, as black as the night sky, twinkle with moisture, similar to the stars.

Her arms fold me into a hug, her skin like ice and as pale as snow. Fee don't retain warmth; as top of the food chain, they don't need it.

I wrap my arms around her, returning the embrace, my brown curls fanning over her shoulders before we release each other. "Erma," I say with a smile ghosting my lips.

She returns the smile, her white teeth gleaming—a stark contrast to the black marble and sky surrounding us. "Come," she says. "We have much to discuss."

Eyeing the group of gatherers near the front gate, she quirks an eyebrow at them. They dip their heads in false respect before we turn, and she ushers me away. I frown, disapproving of the contempt they hold for our creator. Or perhaps, when it comes to Erma, I tend to be more on the protective side. She means more to me than she does to them.

Walking the large expanse of the main room, we come to several archways matching the floor we walk on. The archways appear to be flowing, creating an entrance that looks like black waterfalls.

She steers me to the entrance on our left, the first archway leading to her chambers.

"You've been gone a while, my love. Did you find her?" Erma asks, leading me to a chair built of wood. The surface is unfinished, but the dark grooves and detail of the wood are exceptional and certainly one of a kind. I sit, crossing my shapely legs.

"I did. She has yet to return to her coven, as expected. I believe once a witch is expelled, she isn't allowed to return."

Erma takes a seat in the identical chair across from me, a frown dipping her red-tinted eyebrows in the most adorable way. She places her arms gently on the armrest and leans back. "The question is, why?"

I remain silent. I have no answers for her. This is the same question that's been resurfacing in my head since I found her holed up in her shop with no coven to call her own. I'm protective over Katriane. To see her alone, to witness her inner turmoil and longing, hurts my chest in unexpected ways.

Erma is thoughtful for a moment, her eyes staring off into the distance while she contemplates her question. "What did you say your charge's name was?"

"Kat. Katriane Dupont."

She nods her head, her mind working at such a frantic pace that I can practically see the wheels turning behind her pitch-black eyes.

"A child of Erline, a descendant, tossed from her coven's home," she mumbles aloud, her lips twisting in confusion. Her head flicks back to mine as I imagine her eyes do. It's hard to tell when she's looking at you, and all there is, is black, making it nearly impossible to judge such an action. "This warrants some examination."

Questions form in my head, but before I can ask them, she continues, "A witch out in the open is dangerous. I'm surprised Erline hasn't approached her." She waves her hand. "It's of no matter. Find the girl, watch over her as you see fit, and if you see Erline, tell her to find me. We have much to discuss, she and I. I'd rather not call on her unless it's prudent." Her eyelids narrow, disgust curling her top lip.

Nodding my head, my wet hair sticking to the back of my neck, I bite my tongue to keep from spouting any word of my plans. Erma wouldn't approve.

Erma dips her chin, wordlessly dismissing me. Standing from my chair, I hear it scrape against the marble, the sound ringing my sensitive ears. I grit my teeth and my feathers rustle, agitating their muscles as they attempting to fan away the sound's vibration.

As I turn, I hear Erma clear her throat. I peek over my shoulder, my wet hair sticking to my high cheekbone.

Taking confident steps, she glances out the archway before placing her hands on the back of my arms, gently spinning me back around. Her eyes search mine, but I already know what she wants.

I smile warmly at her before dipping my head and placing a gentle kiss on her lips. Her breasts touch just below mine when she shuffles her body closer. For a moment, she makes herself vulnerable to me before she pulls back, resting her forehead against mine.

Closing her eyes, her words come out in hushed whispers of affection. "Be careful, my love."

I cup her cheek, gently caressing her colorless skin with my thumb before stepping away and releasing her. What I must do would break her like it's breaking me. She would try to stop me, to force me to choose a less dangerous plan. I can't accept that.

Shoving my feelings for Erma aside, I turn back to the archway and exit back into the main gallery, my bare feet stepping soundlessly.

Erma may be my creator, but she's been my lover for as long as I can remember. Our relationship has remained a secret and for good reason. Any sort of display of special treatment would cause an uprising to this group of already unsettled, restless, powerful beings.

I approach the group of conversing, gossiping, angels, and without looking, I know they're staring. "Don't you have work to do?" I growl at them, the words spitting past my lips.

My wings expand, and I flap them twice, lifting my feet off the ground and soaring back through the gate.

****

The rain pounds my face on the mainland of Earth's Realm, obscuring my flight's view. It's still the middle of the night. All the houses I glide over are as dark as the shadows they cast. If I'm going to protect Kat, I'll have to blend in. A walking person with wings would draw far too much attention. The thought of breaking some rules thrills me and propels my actions.

Humans are superstitious in every aspect of life. A simple black cat crosses their path, and they're watching their backs for a witch's scorn. Though on the surface they don't believe, on the inside, they truly do. Erline made them able to sense such things, but over time, they've managed to block the extra senses given to them, deeming them as a spot of insanity.

A demon could lurk in the shadows; they'd feel the eyes on the back of their neck and pass it off as paranoia. It's an extra sense they were built with, but they've chosen to dismiss it. In their mind, if they can't see, feel, or smell it, it simply doesn't exist. It would make the angel's job much easier if they had a shred of self-preservation and trusted the instincts they were given.

I head to my destination—I've passed this place many times. Angling my glide, I reach the ground, my toes curling into the wet grass in front of the deep blue wood shop. The shop is surrounded by pine trees, drenched and dripping, and the path to the small square business is made up of tiny rocks.

Briefly observing for onlookers, I walk forward, my hand outstretched to turn the bass knob on the shop's side door. I grasp it and twist my wrist, but the handle doesn't budge—it's locked. I curse and consider kicking it in, but neighbors are not far, and that would surely cause an unwanted stir. Down the length of the blue siding, a window is placed in the middle.

Chewing the inside of my lip, I contemplate if this is the best move. I walk to the window with catlike steps. The edges are seamless, the building well cared for. My lips thin into a fine line as I come to my decision.

Pulling back my arm, my muscles taut, I pause for a moment before thrusting it forward. My knuckles shatter the glass, the shards cutting into my skin before scattering to the ground faster than the falling rain.

Swiveling my head, I look around before glancing at my knuckles. The sound was much louder than I anticipated, the storm's thunder refusing to work in my favor.

With a pinched pointer finger and thumb, I pull out a few chunks of glass. Black blood seeps from my jagged-edged, frayed skin. Ignoring the punctures, I grip the edge of the window where all the glass is missing, hop once, and jump through, my clothes snagging on the leftover shards still glued in their places.

It's warm in here, the heater humming in the corner, and a tiny pang of guilt forms in my chest. I should turn off the heat before I leave. The Earth Realm is run by currency, and currency is sparse here. These creatures live for their next payment, working like slaves to pay for simple things such as sustenance.

Shrugging, I walk forward to the wall of large power tools, immediately finding the one I need. The metal of the electric saw glints even though there's no light. I stand in front of it, staring, angling my head this way and that before I pick the object from its holder.

It's heavier than I anticipated, the bulk of the weight at the orange plastic handle. I flick the power button, and the machine roars to life, angry and menacing. The small blades instantly pick up speed until they're just a blur, rotating and threatening with their sharp edges.

"What I do for my charges," I mumble, the sound of my voice drowned by the saw.

Thanking Erma for producing us with the absence of pain, I lift the saw over my head and expand my wings from their nestled position against my back. Dripping wet, my pristine feathers look mangled, as if they're privy to my next action.

I take a deep breath and lower the rotating razors to my right wing where it meets skin and muscle along my back. I know they won't regrow. I'm aware that clipping my wings will leave me at half an angel with no ability to return home by my own means. But the job must be done, and sacrifices must be made.

CHAPTER TWO

AIDEN VANDER

EARTH REALM

Swirls of cold, foggy vapor wrap around the ankles of my jeans. I watch as it dips, curls, and sways, caressing the denim like an old friend. It's as if it's alive with a purpose, resembling a desert snake as it slithers through the sand. More fog flows across the cement sprawled under my feet, the light from the street lamps making it glow the finest of shades. My eyes move to my surroundings. I know where I am—I've been here before.

All around me, tucked between old brick buildings, are empty streets and sidewalks. This is the path I take on my way home. No sounds of trains, horns, or incessant chatter . . . nothing reaches my ears besides my own lumbering movements.

The area is vacant of people, of flowing life and walking shoes. It's like I'm the only person on the planet. I grunt as I plod ahead. This isn't normal. Where the hell are all the people?

It's cold here, wherever here is. Though I recognize where I am, I know that I'm not in reality. People don't just disappear as if they never existed in the first place. In reality, these streets can be quiet, but there's always one person walking them, or a car driving by, or someone shouting out their apartment window. I'll be damned if I believe that suddenly nothing existing is normal. I'm many things, but a fool isn't one of them.

The slight breeze raises pinpricks and goosebumps across my skin, and my breath mists out in front of me. With each step, I get a little angrier. The emptiness creeps me out.

I glance up to the blanket of dark, billowing clouds covering the night sky, hiding the stars and the shine of the moon. I can't deny that it's peaceful here—no trouble arises; there's no tendril of life's chaotic drama. The disorganized mess of our world's stress doesn't hide in the dark, waiting to be unraveled and triggering pointless, unrelenting fret.

The scent of rain is in the air, tickling the inside of my nose with its fresh, crisp odor. I lift my hand and scrub my nostrils with the heel of my palm. Even though I know this is only a dream, I pause to bask in how real everything feels.

I've been here before, in this dream. Each time, it's the same . . . but different.

For the past few nights, every time I fall asleep, this is where my dreams take me. Like a welcoming –friend—a wanted guest hosted by the frigid fog that clears a little more with each dream. My sleeping state paints the picture of my surroundings in detail. I'm sure if I were to reach out and run my hand across the brick, I'd feel the sharp edges as it scrapes across my fingertips.

And she's always here . . . always appearing, transparent yet motherly and loving in presence. I find it slightly annoying. She's a persistent visitor to this reoccurring dream. I know without a doubt that if I turn around and face that alleyway, she'll be there, waiting for me with no answers.

I steel myself, tensing the muscles between my shoulder blades, and turn to face her. The fog and mist scatter, its caress disturbed by my shift. I know she's there. She's always there.

Keeping my eyes down and my hood over my head, I wait until I see the pale yellow of her thick socks. They look like the ones I got in the hospital during my stay after I received a severe concussion—what can I say . . . boxing has its hazards. Is that what this is? My warped brain having a little fun?

My teeth clench, an audible grind as they scrape against each other, and I raise my vision. The realistic, transparent figure that she is makes me nervous for the unknown. I don't like things I can't prove with fact. Dreams aren't based on fact; no, they're twisted with snips of reality and fear.

She wears a nightdress—the kind a mother would wear after tucking the covers under their young's tiny chins, safely snuggling them inside their beds before they fall fast asleep. It's floral-printed in pink, buttoned up the front and a petaled, cream-colored collar around the neck. I reach that transparent slope above her shoulder, just above the collar, where a gold cross dangles from a delicate chain. And finally, I see her subtle white teeth behind her sincere, maternal smile and her warm, comforting eyes.

This is how she always greets me. Her friendliness irks me; it's something I'm not used to, something I've never had directed at me before.

I see the alleyway through her. The old brick walls create a narrow, unlit path.

"Aiden," she whispers as if she's happy to see me. As if I'm her son, and I've just come home for a visit. My teeth grind again.

I've never spoken to her. This is a dream, right? Why would I speak to a figure my brain conjured? I clear my throat and shift my weight.

Lowering my hood, I consider her with speculating eyes. Chewing the inside of my lip, I take a chance. If my dreams keep taking me here, it's time to figure out why. "Who are you?"

Her smile grows wider; the twinkle in her eyes sparkles with moisture. How is it possible for a dream to be so vivid?

As a boxer, I'm trained to notice subtle movements. I recognize the nervous gesture when she takes a step forward, her slender hands clasped together in front of her as her fingers knot themselves. "I'm Jane."

"Jane . . ." I say slowly, my throat thick with confusion. The hood of my sweatshirt rubs against my nape as I tilt my head to the side. "What do you want?"

She blinks, the corners of her lips slope, and her throat constricts like she's just swallowed a marble. When she finally speaks, the tone of her voice is heavy, lower, and full of an emotion that doesn't fit her previous mood. "You'll soon find out."

Her fingers twist faster, harder, before she drops them to her side with more force than necessary and closes the distance between us.

Folding me into a hug, her hands rest on my tense shoulder blades. It's a warm hug though it shouldn't be—she's not real. She's transparent.

This is only a dream, *I chant inside my head.*

The warmth seeps through my clothes, my skin, my muscles and bones. I close my eyes for a moment, relishing the feeling of so much unconditional love inside one simple, common gesture . . . so much comfort—the very thing I've lacked my entire life. It feels foreign, and a part of me bucks against it.

The tugging sensation, the one I always feel before I wake against my will, yanks on my abdomen. My time here is over, my dream finished.

43

She rests her chin on the top of my shoulder as I stand still as a statue, waiting for the pull to take me away. The scent of oncoming rain and her skin combine, smelling of fresh roses after a spring thunderstorm.

"Save the girl," she whispers.

****

My eyelids hesitate before they open, my eyes searching the dimly lit ceiling of my basic apartment bedroom. Morning's rays of sunshine shimmer through my thin, holey curtains.

I blink, remembering her warm embrace, her tender touch . . . her *words*. 'Save the girl,' echoes in my head once more, leaving me with questions I may never have answers to.

What girl? A girlfriend? I don't have one.

Sitting up, I swing my legs over the edge of the mattress before glancing at the brown, carpet-covered floor that scrubs against my bare toes. I rub my eyes with stiff fingers, clearing the sticky layer of sleep from them.

My white sheet lays in a tangled mess across the scruff surface of the old carpet. Some horns honk, vibrating against the tall buildings outside and spilling in through my thin glass windows. I cringe, my neck muscles straining against the abrupt noise at such an early hour. It's the sound—the evidence—of the waking city's impatient citizens as they rush to work a few minutes too late.

My eyes search the wall across from me, the brown and white pinstriped wallpaper peeling back from its seams, just like my own pathetic life. I see nothing but the dream replaying over and over. It felt so real, the details so vivid.

Testing my weight, I stand and travel the length of my small apartment for a bottle of water.

KATRIANE DUPONT

EARTH REALM

I straighten the contents on the wooden shelves nailed against the wall in the back, lifting the raven feathers, the toadstool, the dried poppy seeds. Potions in a variety of different colors swirl inside their corked glass bottles to my left. I ignore the potions, vowing to dust them later, and shimmy to my right, propped up on my tippy-toes. I swipe my rag across the shelf before pausing and glancing at the speck-free mirror in front of me.

Exhaustion is etched around my brown eyes. My black pixie haircut is stiff from products and styled just the way I like it. That's the thing about short hair—it takes only a handful of minutes to dishevel it the way I want it. A small, almost invisible, nose ring is pinched against my nostril, and a few, barely visible freckles dance across the bridge of my nose. My nose is short, narrow, plain. My cheekbones sit high and protruding.

My eyes shift from one to the other, seeing the loneliness so evident inside them. I have no coven, and that can lead any witch to a small bout of stress and depression.

I lift my hand and trace the dark circles under my eyes with my fingertips, settling back on my heels. "Sweet, holy mother of . . .," I mumble my curse. My vulnerability is causing this evidence of lack of sleep.

A few months ago, I made a deal with Erline, Fee of the Earth Realm. The Fee are powerful beings, each one charged with a different realm. Unlike everyone else on the Earth Realm, witches are descendants of the First Born, Erline's biological daughter, Myla.

A long time ago, it is said that Erline grew lonely—she wanted a child of her own. She'd watched her realm, watched all she created reproduce, and she longed for the same. Erline and her once lover, Kheelan, the Fee of Death Realm, 'bounced in the bed,' and a few months later, out popped Myla, the First Born witch. We're told she had wondrous powers beyond imagination. And each of her daughters were given a sliver of it . . . insert the Witches.

When I made the deal - when I cured the Red Death - Astrid, the High Priestess of my coven, banned me, sent me packing, and effectively disowned me. Summoning Erline is forbidden and unforgivable. I knew those rules going into that meeting with our maker. But a witch without a coven suffers because she has no one. No one to lean on, no one to discuss their ways, no one to turn to for guidance and protection.

My brown eyes glow a neon orange around the rims. She, the being I now share my body with, reminds me that I'm not alone, reminds me of the price I paid. I close my eyes and tilt my head away from the mirror. I have yet to accept sharing my body.

The private office of my little witch shop, Lunaire, serves as my altar room. I'm an obsessive cleaner—when I fret, I dust and organize.

My mother, Janine, always told me to keep my hands busy when senseless thoughts clogged my mind. There isn't a speck of dust to be seen, but still I lift each item, each instrument, and wipe them down with my microfiber cloth. The upside to fretting is at least everything is spotless and streak-free. So, I've got that going for me.

A light from my left catches my eye, and I tilt my head in its direction. Placed on my wooden altar table, smack dab in the middle of the room, my white crystal glows. The crystal is round, smooth, and partially see through. Inside, swirls of white sparkle and turn—those swirls now glow a brilliant shade of white.

The light hum coming from its center as it vibrates against the wood focuses as a secondary alert. The spell works to perfection, as by my design, alerting me that someone has entered my shop.

At least it's the white crystal. If the red crystal next to it glows, I know it's something other than human.

I fold the cloth, lay it on my desk, and exit my office, closing the door gently behind me. My footsteps echo through the small hallway, passing by the small break room that holds my beloved brewing coffee, as I head to the main area of my shop. Smiling a greeting at my potential customers, I give a cheerful welcome. "Welcome to Lunaire. If there's anything you can't find, let me know."

The two humans nod their thanks and head over to the collection of feathered dreamcatchers against the wall.

This little town is full of supernatural speculations, suspicions, and history. Many moons ago, witches were hung just a few blocks down the road. Some of them were just accused witches, not actually the real deal, but those moments in history still make quite a stir. The supernatural and paranormal lovers flock to this town like flies to cow shit.

On the outside, tourists come for the history, but on the inside, they believe they'll get some kind of divine, freaky-deaky, sneak peek at what's really going on behind the curtain. Of course, their assumptions are correct, but I guarantee none of them will see anything that'll crown their interest. Not unless you count the few shops and museums this town has to offer.

Humans aren't bad, but they tend to fear what they can't explain. The supernatural live under the radar, and we're quite good at it—years of adapting and surviving under the noses of suspicion will do that. Even the shifters keep a low profile, remaining in their territory and only leaving when necessary. Though we are top of the food-chain, there are more humans than supernaturals. Even a single lion can't fight off a herd of angry gazelle.

For these sorts of tourists, little shops like mine make a killing during the fall season. Everyone seems so fascinated with magic, searching for a little spook to feed their curiosity. It's not like it's a new thing. Dreamcatchers, tarot cards, Ouija boards, herbal remedies . . . they've been around for years, and many humans use them, even though they don't get very far. Though, I've heard a few have summoned demons by accident.

I mentally shrug. There's no helping the notoriously curious. What did my mother used to say? Oh yes. Curiosity killed the cat, but captivation brought it back.

"How much is this?" the petite blond customer asks, shifting her body and holding up an object.

Standing behind the counter, I squint my eyes to read the title of the large paperback book. The galaxy's stars sprinkled across the glossy surface. "*Theories Below the Surface*," I read aloud. "Excellent choice."

I give her the price, and she looks at the cover once more. Smiling a giddy grin, she tucks the book into the wedge of her elbow and continues browsing with her friend. The title is self-explanatory, and the contents are close to accurate.

Whoever wrote that book had great knowledge of what this universe holds.

The doorbell jingles again, and I glance at the door. The rain still downpours, beating everything in its path. The tropical storm wreaks havoc in our area. A puddle forms on the carpet just inside the door. It's a defiant storm, and somehow, I find myself enjoying it, puddles and all. The smell of wet earth reaches my nose, and I inhale the aroma, taking a moment to bask in it—the smell of freedom and regrowth.

A small figure steps through the door wearing a dark green poncho dribbled in drops of precipitation. Shaking the beads off the hood, feminine hands lift it back before blue eyes glance around the shop. A curtain of brown hair cascades to her shoulders with wide curls. She's breathtaking, with natural, full red lips and perfect, symmetrical bone structure. I instantly envy her.

In my peripheral vision, both women turn and stare at the new customer. The brown-haired female shakes the droplets from the rest of her poncho and walks up to me, her steps confident and purposeful.

"Welcome," I say, pasting a smile on my face. "What can I help you with?"

She props an elbow on the glass surface and leans into the counter. Her eyes wander around the place before a small smirk plays against the corners of her mouth. "I'm looking for a job." She returns her bright blue eyes to mine.

I double blink, thrown by her forward attitude. "A job?"

She dips her head, her curls bouncing. Her movements seem forced, like she's used to standing as still as a statue. She's cold natured, the smile on her face false. "Are you hiring?"

I take a moment to think while blowing out a breath through 'o' shaped lips. "I wasn't originally, but . . .," I bite my bottom lip. Her large, almond-shaped eyes plead with mine. "Yeah." I nod, coming to a final decision. "Yeah, I can use the help." If anything, I can use the company.

Her features relax, and a ghost of a smile plays at the corners of her mouth. It's like I'm staring at an angel. I frown. It should be sinful to be that beautiful.

"It's settled," she whispers through pearly white teeth. "When can I start?"

I clear my throat and shift my gaze to my browsing customers. Anything to look away from those alluring eyes that are making me so comfortable. I don't swing for women, but her presence seems to suck you right in. "Well, we should probably have an interview. If you wait just a moment," I answer, nodding my head toward the customers heading our way, "I'll have some free time to chat with you."

She captures her bottom lip with her top teeth, and the muscles between her eyebrows tense, forming a few lines. "Yes. Yes, of course."

As the two women approach, she backs away from the counter to a nearby shelf, browsing the books on display. I feel my lips tighten while ringing up the customers' items. My attention flits between the register and the possible future employee. As a witch with no protection, I've made it a rule to never trust strangers.

You have a right to be leery, she says. I jump at the voice inside my head, my shoulders bunching and irritating the muscle knots in my neck.

She doesn't speak to me often, but when she does, it's always her version of wisdom. As an act of stubbornness, I have yet to respond to her. I don't even know if I can. I may be a strong witch, but telepathy has never been a gift I've possessed.

I clear my throat again, ignoring the curious glances from the two customers, and tell them their total. The blond customer digs for change inside her pink, polka dot wallet, counting the pennies, nickels, and dimes. She pauses when the stranger barks out a chorus of laughter, and our heads swivel back to where she stands.

Holding a book between boney fingers, she flips through the pages, her eyes scanning the words. I glance at the cover—*Spells of Love* is the title. I wonder what she finds so funny. . .

I hand the two girls their plastic bags of purchased items, my old witch coven's crescent on the side—a half moon with a strike through it. I adopted the crescent as my shop's logo, finding the thrill in the situation of possible discovery. They mumble their thank you's and turn to leave. The door chimes as they head back into the rain before darting to their car.

The stranger approaches me, book in hand. "Is this accurate?" she asks, still flipping through the pages with a smile on her face.

My shoulders bob as I shrug. "I wouldn't know. I've never attempted a love spell."

Her eyes meet mine. "You're a wit- err . . . someone who practices magic?" she asks, but the words seem automatic, like there isn't a lick of curiosity behind them. Her tone is cold, just as her false smile, void of real emotion.

I purse my lips, the voice inside my head's words coming back to me. "Yes," I answer simply.

"Does it ever work?" She flips another page over.

Gulping, I decide to lie. "No."

She gives me a considerate look before placing the book on the counter. She holds out her hand to me. "Tember," she says.

I frown, taking her hand in mine and firmly shaking while remembering my manners. "Tember?" I question.

"As in, *Sep*-tember." She dips her head but keeps her eyes on mine.

My eyebrows slope farther toward my eyes. "Were you born in September?"

Tember takes her hand back and props her elbow back against the glass counter. "No."

I twitch my nose, my lips momentarily twisting to the side. *All right then.* "Katriane," I introduce myself, "but everyone calls me Kat."

She nods her head once, a greeting of sorts.

Walking out from behind the counter, I come to stand just in front of her, stuffing my fingers into my back pockets and rocking on my heels. "So, I suppose we should start with identification and the last place you worked."

Tember pauses from standing upright, her eyes widening the slightest. "I-" She clears her throat. "I don't have any."

I double blink, my lashes brush my cheek against my pinched face. "Oh. You're looking for something more . . . under the table?"

Nodding, she holds her confidence. She should be nervous; anyone would be nervous. If you're asking for employment and don't have any form of identification, a normal person would be frightened they'd be turned in or at least anxious about being turned down. She seems to display neither.

I wipe a hand over my face. How am I supposed to check this girl out? What if she's a criminal, and I wake up in the morning with nothing in the cash register and no name to give the police?

My hand drops to my side, and I inhale a sharp breath. "All right. There's only one way to do this then."

Her head tilts to the side, freeing the curls from behind her shoulder. I crook my finger for her to follow me. Against my better judgment, I turn my back to her and begin walking to my back office.

"Do what, exactly?" she asks, a hint of curiosity in her voice.

"Have a chat in private, of course," I say, pushing the door open and entering my office.

CHAPTER THREE

AIDEN VANDER

EARTH REALM

My biceps contract before my fist swings, connecting with the bag dangling from the low ceiling. It sways and twirls, just like the fog and mist of my dreams. I punch it with more force than necessary, my thoughts plaguing my actions. My taped hands take the true beating of my unrelenting frustration and anxiety. How much I wish this was a person and not just a black bag filled with sand.

Beading sweat dribbles down my back, picking up speed after it travels over each flexing muscle, and dipping to the curve of my lower back. It soaks into the elastic of my boxing shorts, creating an uncomfortable rubbing sensation.

One. Two. One. Two. I chant to myself, counting each hit to the bag, desperately trying to concentrate on what's in front of me . . . of what's real.

"Aiden!" a familiar shout comes from behind me. My stomach lurches as I'm torn away from my concentration. I whip my head around, stopping the swing of the bag with one hand.

My boxing coach, Frank, approaches with a clipboard in hand as he scans the contents across the crisp pages. He was once a boxing champion and a good choice for a manager. I was lucky he ran across me when he did.

I was a scraper, continuously getting in trouble everywhere I went. I like to think that trouble always finds me, no matter where I hide, and not the other way around.

One day, I got into a fight in the street, protecting a homeless man from a pair of bullies who found it fun to pick on the less fortunate. Frank happened to be walking by. As he approached our brawl, the presence of another person scared off the perps. He saw something in me that day and took me under his wing, giving me a purpose I'd never had.

For a kid who grew up in the foster system, the hope he had presented me was welcoming. But now, his persistence was irritating, grating on every ounce of patience I possess. He's a slave driver, even though I know he does everything to better me, to give me a future I couldn't possibly get on my own.

I wipe the sweat from my forehead with the white towel draped over my neck. My eyebrows lift before I begin questioning. "Yeah?" I ask, my throat dry from heavy breathing.

Lifting the bottled water that sits on the floor, I notice it leaves behind a pool of condensation, and I take a generous gulp. The cold liquid quenches my parched throat and cools my heated nerves.

"You have a fight Friday." He flicks his eyes to mine. A sparse layer of red eyelashes blink at me.

My eyebrows bunch together, and a bead of sweat drips from the movement. Tensing my lips, I ask, "With who? I didn't know there was one." My voice is deep, intimidating to most who don't know me.

Lines develop over his forehead when his eyes widen. "With Jim, The Reaper." He places the clipboard under his arm and twists his lips in a mocking gesture. "Why? Do you have plans Friday night? Big, bad Aiden can't make it?" His voice dips lower. "Pussy-whipped by his girl?"

Blinking slowly at him, I bite my tongue to keep from lashing back with unnecessary words. I pull the towel from my neck and clear away the beaded dew on the side of my water bottle, busying my eyes and fingers. "No," I rumble, before mumbling, "I just wasn't expecting it."

A date with a girl would be out of the question, even if I had a girl to call my own. I don't date—I have no time. My time isn't my own; it belongs to Frank and this sorry excuse for a gym.

Someday. Someday I'll find the right one and leave this place for a better tomorrow. Grateful as I may be, I know this career won't last forever.

Frank's beady eyes narrow as he sets the mockery aside. "You know how ruthless The Reaper can be." He pauses, considering my lack of interest. "You ready for it?"

I glance up at him and take one more swig. My love for this sport is gone. Vanished. Overdone. But I can't quit now. I'm close to making something of myself—so close to being something more than that nobody passing by strangers on the street, thanks to Frank. "Yeah," I say after I swallow.

The Reaper is known for his ruthlessness. Just last year, he killed a man with one punch. It's how he earned his boxing name.

Frank slaps me on the back, the sting on my wet skin causing my jaw to flex. "Good." He laughs. "Head on home. I'll see ya tomorrow." Frank turns before calling over his shoulder, "Bright and early, Aiden."

Watching him walk away, I wait a moment, my jaw continuing its rhythmic flex to the beat of my pounding heart, to my impatience. I sigh through my nose and head to the locker room. My sneakers squeak against the gym floor and echo throughout the building.

Turning the corner, the smell of old socks, similar to corn chips, forces me to swallow a gag. I eye my gym bag sitting on the worn, wooden bench inside the locker room, right where I left it. I pick my jeans and hooded sweatshirt from inside, change my clothes at a slow pace, and dream of a future I may never have.

ELIZA PLAATS

EARTH REALM

"Mrs. Tiller, you need this surgery," I beg, my eyes remain unblinking as I try to convince my patient from across the conference table.

I fidget in my seat. I'm crossing a line, taking this conversation a step further. It feels as though I'm forcing her to do an elective procedure that I know she needs to save her life. However, this must be her choice and hers alone. As her doctor, I can try to convince my patient, but I can't scare her into doing anything. It's tough to balance the patient's needs against what's best for her. That doesn't mean the words aren't on the tip of my tongue and occasionally cross it.

In trembling hands, her plump fingers fidget with the pamphlet I just gave her. Her red-rimmed eyes roam over the letters of this hospital's name—Mercy Memorial Hospital—while her husband pats her back in a soothing gesture. My mind flicks through possible things to say, anything to convince her I'm right without pushing my agenda. I come up short, lacking in a bedside manner that my job normally requires. Clearing my throat, I shift in my seat once more, my uncomfortable attitude becoming smothering, clogging the words in my throat.

My patient, Mrs. Tiller, has been here many times, weighing the options of proceeding with this surgery. She's scared and rightfully so. Any surgery is dangerous. Each time she attends these meetings, she has new questions. Though she is desperate for other options, she's been reluctant about the Gastric Bypass surgery even though it was her family's recommendation. She's getting up there in age. Losing the weight by using other means has been difficult for her. Her bones, her body, no longer hold the youth she once had. She has foster children to chase after. She needs this surgery.

I glance at Dr. Cassandra Grant sitting next to me, the fellow surgeon on my team. Her back is straight, her posture perfect. She has no qualms about emotional states like I do. I have enough problems in my own life to know better than to add others to it. Not a line of stress mars her mahogany-colored skin. Her afro is beautiful, a perfect sphere. It must take her hours to maintain it.

I look back over the conference table top, back to Mrs. Tiller. I can taste her anxiety from where I sit, heightening my own.

"It will save your life," I blurt, my voice far from reassuring. I clear my throat and try again, flattening my hand against the tabletop. "You've tried everything to lose the weight. Now it's your turn to trust us. We can help you."

Cassandra leans forward, the cushion of her chair letting out air as she does. "Gastric Bypass does have its risks, but as your doctors, we're confident that the surgery will go without a hitch."

Mrs. Tiller lifts her tear-filled eyes and meets my gaze. I keep my face sincere and hopeful, giving her a light smile of reassurance though it feels more as a grimace. The emotions in the air are smothering; I don't know how no one else seems unaffected by it.

"Will you consent to the surgery?" I ask, the toe of my sneaker tapping the floor.

Mr. Tiller looks from me to his wife. I can see in his eyes which option he wants her to take. He wants her to live, to be healthy and happy, and this is how he believes it is to be fixed. It helps to have rooted and supportive family on the side of a doctor's opinion.

His features are memorable. Like an old hound dog. He's worn with age and has heavy bags under his eyes. Mr. Tiller operates the trains in town and often works long hours. I'm surprised he hasn't retired yet.

In my early thirties, I have learned one thing. Weight, vanity, health—it means nothing. Love. Love is the reason for living. It is also the very thing I lack, the gaping hole in my chest, the thing that keeps me up at night and the thing I actively avoid. I'm alone, and it's constantly dangled in front of my face, filling me with a sense of desperate envy. It causes me to be scared of it, to fight the urge to run the opposite direction every time it's presented as a possible option.

If Mrs. Tiller wishes to live and love another day, her best option is to choose life—to choose the surgery. It isn't my job to force the option, however. It's my job to guide. That's what I keep chanting inside my head.

To my relief, she nods before wiping the streams of tears from her cheek with careless swipes. I breathe a sigh of relief, my red hair fanning my face. I lift my hand to scratch the itch, watching her large frame shake in fear and with good reason. Surgery is always risky, especially when you have everything to lose.

I lean back in my seat, my lips pressed in a hard line. Instead of feeling happy, butterflies beat against the inside of my stomach, their flutters ones of anger and regret.

CHAPTER FOUR

KATRIANE DUPONT

EARTH REALM

Once in my office, I turn and crook my finger again, producing a thin smile. "In here," I call a little too loud. I'm nervous about having someone back here. This space is usually only visited by myself. An anxious chuckle threatens to escape. I'm placing myself in such a vulnerable position, despite ignoring the little voice in my head that warned me a few minutes ago to be leery.

Tember follows me in and glances around at the magical objects and potions. "Interesting," she mumbles.

As she walks over to the shelf I previously dusted, she bumps her hip against the altar table before she has time to pick up one of the swirling green potions—my potions, my stuff. A small bout of possession bubbles inside me. *Mine.*

Her continuous curiosity isn't what has my attention though. What has my attention is the glowing crystal. Not the white one, the red one. It glows like a beacon in the room. The breath seizes in my throat.

She's not human, she mumbles with a smidge of smug attitude, as if I should already know this. As if I needed her input to understand the situation I put myself in.

For a split moment, my heart sinks to my toes. Her earlier warning comes back to haunt me, echoing in my head and sending regret to replace my forced optimistic attitude.

I feel my face darken to that of a true witch's nature. The nerves pinch as the skin contorts, the area surrounding my eyes feeling heavy and full of pressure. In the mirror of my peripheral vision, my eyes darken around the lids to pitch-black skin, my teeth point to tipped ends, and my eyes glow around the rims of my irises. The neon glow still startles me. The glowing isn't my nature—it's hers. Her beast.

Witches have to chant words to produce a spell. Fortunately, I gained *her* extra abilities, making me not like most witches. My hands lift from my sides and fling out in front of me, palms facing Tember.

Tember's hair whips to the side, her head tilting toward me as she's flung into the nearby wall and pinned there. A few vials crash to the ground, some sizzling on the wooden floor as the liquid spills out, seeping over tiny shards of glass. Tapping into the powers of *her* has aided me since our merge. I shouldn't do it. I should pretend she doesn't exist, but sometimes her power is hard to resist. Especially when it comes with its own set of benefits.

"What are you doing?" Tember snarls, her lip curled as she struggles against the wall she's pinned against. She glances up at me, her narrowed eyes now wide with shock.

I stalk in her direction, heavy footsteps against the wood floor echoing throughout the small room. "What are you?" I growl, my hand still suspended in the air, holding her in place.

"I'm not anything." Her voice is dead, void of emotion, causing disbelieving thoughts to form in my head. "Your eyes . . ." she comments, double blinking. "Have they always done that?"

"Bullshit." The word comes from deep in my throat, resembling a deep baritone. I ignore her question, demanding answers instead. "Tell me what you are."

She glares at me, a challenge in her stare and completely unaltered by my hostile attitude. "I'm human."

I scoff, shaking my head in a slow motion. Does she really expect me to believe this? The evidence glowing inside that red crystal says otherwise. "A human would never say that." Shifting my head, I point it in the direction of the crystal before returning my darkened, glowing eyes to her. "My handy supernatural detector says you're not. Tell me, or I'll provide you with a one-way ticket to hell."

Steady now, she says. My nose twitches at her order, but I take a calming breath anyway.

Tember's glare remains the same, blatant and unfearful. I take a step closer, a few inches from her face, hoping to scare her enough to speak the words I ask. I should have known better than to take a step closer. I should have kept the distance. Judgment has never been my strong suit.

The whites and color of her eyes disappear, replaced with one solid shade of bright gold. The color glows until it's blinding enough that I have to squint. It creates a circling halo around her head and her face remains angelic as she reaches forward. Her lips apply pressure against mine, and my eyes grow wide. I force them to remain open, shock crossing my features.

My skin quivers, a light gold glow seeps out of my pores and straight into hers. The sensation is caressing, like a lover's gentle touch, feather-light, and raises goosebumps on my skin. Guilt fills my soul, rolling my insides, consuming me with such an overwhelming and misplaced fault. Revulsion swirls in the pit of my stomach, self-loathing the cause. My face relaxes, my features return to more human than otherworldly as the energy leaves my body.

I'm drowning. I'm drowning in a pit of sorrow and self-loathing.

Resist, she orders.

Her words are enough to cause coherent thoughts, like she replaced my own subconscious with her voice. My hand drops to my side, breaking the hold on Tember. I rip my lips from hers, a grimace on my face, angry despite the lingering effects of doubt and guilt that remain. Stumbling back, I wipe my mouth with the back of my hand using more force than necessary, keeping my eyes on her.

Angel, she whispers, providing me with the answers I need. *A creation of Fee Erma.*

"You're an angel," I growl, my fingers balling into fists. I resist the urge to spit on my clean floor, wanting to dispel the last effects of the lip-lock. "That was the Angel's Kiss."

An Angel's Kiss is meant to fill its victims with so much self-doubt that for a human, it takes but one peck to be suicidal. It's a useful tool for the angels, but I've only ever heard about it.

Angels aren't always filled with light. They can be either trustworthy or untrustworthy. Most are known to be propelled by their own wants and desires. It's better to be leery of them, even if they seem to have good intentions. They're immortal, living for hundreds of years unless someone manages to kill them. It is said they wear their heart on their sleeve. I wonder if that's metaphorical. How old is this angel standing before me?

Tember's hands are placed on her knees, bent over and breathing deep while peeking at me through her curls fanned across her face. Her eyes dim back to their normal blue, but she doesn't answer my statement.

"I've never met an angel." I stand up straight and wipe my mouth one more time. My eyes narrow and my chin juts to the side. "What do you want?"

She straightens her spine and stands to her full height, the poncho crackling as she moves. Her shoulders still rising and falling, she answers in huffed breaths, "You shouldn't be that strong. Your eyes shouldn't glow." She pauses until her eyes narrow just as mine. "What have you done?"

I square my shoulders, my mind working at a frantic pace, grasping for a lie—any lie. "I haven't done anything."

She takes a step forward. "Is this why your coven disowned you?"

I double blink, the narrowing of my eyes relaxing and crease-free. "How do—"

A snarl rips from her throat, cutting me off. "How do I know? You're my charge, Kat."

Chewing the inside of my lip, I think this over. If she's my Guardian, why wasn't she looking out for me when I was in those woods? When I was making a deal that altered my life and connected me to another soul—a beast? "Where are your wings?" I blurt.

Crossing her arms, she answers quickly with a clipped tone, "Disposed of."

"You clipped your wings?" Why would an angel dispose of the only thing that can take them home? What could she possibly be doing here? I've never heard of an angel willingly clipping her wings.

She ignores me, considering my choice of clothes. "You're vulnerable, Kat. The least you can do is dress less conspicuously. Try not to stand out . . ."

I follow her eyes down to my holey skinny jeans. They disappear into ankle length, front tying, leather boots. My shit-kickers, I like to call them. To match the pants, I'm wearing a black, almost see-through, sleeveless shirt, my tattoo-covered arms visible and complimenting the outfit. I thought I had chosen well, but I've always had a twisted sense of fashion.

She's right. Most witches remain off the radar, never displaying any kind of show for attention. Anything to keep us from wandering eyes and curious ears that could end with burning our bodies to a crisp against a wooden post. My mother—and most of the coven—wear dresses and boring ones at that. Outfits no one would give a second glance to, often in bland colors. *Hide your nature*, my mother would always say, the double meaning never eluding me.

I lift my head to her, my expression blank. What I wear is nobody's business, not even my angel's. "You didn't answer my question. What do you want?"

Her stare remains unwavering, blinking only when necessary. The pause in her response makes me nervous, and I shift my weight from one foot to the other. "I'm here for you, Kat. You'll give me a job so I can watch over you."

I internally buck against her order. This woman has balls, demanding things of me as if I'm a child in need of guidance. "Why?"

Tember leans against the wall she was just pinned against, keeping her arms folded over her chest. "The only person I know of who had glowing neon eyes was Myla. Do you know who Myla is?"

I look away from her, the guilt returning and riding my back like a rodeo queen.

"That's what I thought." She pushes off the wall with her shoulder and walks to me, grabbing my chin in her hands and forcing my eyes to meet hers. She searches their depths, and I feel Myla surface through my eyes. Tember glares. "What have you done, Kat," she accuses me.

I rip my head from her grasp and divert the question with a rude tone. "Do you have anywhere to stay?"

Tember's jaw ticks before she answers, "No."

"I live upstairs," I begin.

"I know."

I clear my throat, her tension stifling. I feel like I'm being berated by my mother. "There's a couch . . ."

She nods her head once, understanding the meaning behind my words. Even I know a wingless angel can't walk the street. After all, she can't go home. "Thoughtful, I don't sleep."

DYSON COLEMAN

DEATH REALM

Without purpose, I kick a stray stone as I walk the large path, my hands folded behind my back and my face downcast. It's paved with white, worn bricks, just like the walls rising up the sides, towering over until you can no longer see them. They're filled with windowless rooms for the dead. The path is large enough to hold several vehicles, but there's nothing of the sort here.

I'm a tinkerer. I keep my hands busy. Or I used to, anyway. With nothing here, I have no purpose. I walk the streets, aimlessly, my thoughts constantly switching to my previous life.

The Death Realm is a city built of stone. There are endless rows of buildings that look like they belong to the medieval time period. I snort, finding it fitting. A cruel leader and void-of-any-emotion Realm.

Several shades pass me, a few nodding their heads while others ignore all that's around them.

Up the way, I see shades held in Electro-Triangles—a torture device that holds shades inside, tormenting them with painful electricity bolts. It's what Chad was referring to—how the vampires have other ways to get to us.

Their moans of pain are constant, their expressions twisted with agony. Vampires lean against a wall, their arms folded as they watch with intense interest and sickening fascination. I don't know what these shades are being punished for, but Kheelan, the Fee of this realm, often doesn't have a reason. He lets his vampires do what they want, and punishments are delivered for the simplest of crimes or sometimes just for the sick satisfaction that they can punish without cause.

I continue what I'm doing, aimlessly roaming about and kicking stray pebbles fallen from the crumbling walls while ignoring the torture just up the way. Hatred fills me, but I try desperately to shove it aside. This isn't right. This isn't what death should be like.

The stone under my feet should grit against my shoe. My body is ready, prepared for the subtle vibrations, but it never comes. At least I can still smell. The air is perfumed with a musky scent, like moss or mold, and no breeze helps carry it away.

Filling my thoughts with my wolf, I try to convince him to see reason. I can feel him huddled in a ball inside me, and every time I try to coax some response, I get nothing. No perking of the ears, no clawing at my insides, no emotion. It's like he's trying not to exist. Being a wolf-shifter, it's hard for me when my other half shows no interest in his existence, even in the afterlife.

A hand is placed on my shoulder the same moment words reach my ears. "Dyson?" a nervous, feminine voice says.

I turn around, my shoes making no noise against the rough surface. When you're a shade, passing through things, being soundless, comes naturally.

Jane and Tanya stand there, their teeth showing through wide smiles. They look at the punishment happening behind me, those smiles wavering for a split second before forcing them to return. I quirk an eyebrow at Jane before settling my eyes on Tanya.

Taking my hands from behind my back, I place them on my hips before nervously looking around. "How'd it go?"

"Can we," she whispers and glances around, "can we talk somewhere private?"

I nod once, feeling a bit relieved to walk away from the sight behind me. "Yeah. Jane? Your room is close by. Do you mind?"

Jane nods and turns on her yellow sock-covered heel. We follow her a few feet before she steps right, her body passing right through a wall. Tanya follows, and I after.

The stone tickles as it passes through me. It's the same feeling as dropping a hundred feet on a ride at an amusement park. It's not my favorite feeling in the world—my stomach rolling, my organs feeling as though they're in my throat, my chest aching. I imagine if it were still necessary for me to breathe, it'd seize the oxygen and hold it hostage. I count my blessings though. I could be one of those shades forced to endure torture in the Electro-Triangle.

Emerging on the other side, Jayne and Tanya turn toward me. Jane's minimal furnishings—a small couch and a rug—are visible through their bodies.

We aren't allowed much. The dead can't take anything with them, and we don't receive anything when we get here. If we could, I imagine Jane would have this room filled with knitting objects or clay masterpieces. She seems like the crafty type.

"I believe Aiden will come willingly. Are you sure Reaper's Breath will aid his passage?" Jane asks.

I bunch my shoulders in a sloppy shrug before rubbing my jaw. "I have no reason not to believe it will. It seems to know what we want before we voice it."

Jane bobbles in a nervous nod, her fingers twisting together.

Turning to Tanya, I ask, "And you're sure he'll join us? In the rebellion?" She nods her head, but I'm distracted by Jane and her nervous energy. "Jane?"

Her lips turned downward. "It's my turn to ask for a favor."

I sigh and run my hand down my face. Why does everyone want things from me?

ELIZA PLAATS

EARTH REALM

Cassandra hands me a paper cup full of hot, steaming, black brew. The smell reaches my nose, settling my insides and the dark feeling there. My insides feel twisty. I can't shake the feeling that I'm going to regret pushing Mrs. Tiller.

Mrs. Tiller agreed to the surgery. She's choosing life, which should have eased my fear for her. But instead, it heightened; just the opposite. It's rare for me to have feelings for others. I avoid it at all cost, but I've come to know Mrs. Tiller and her family. They're good people, and once you grow attached to a patient, emotions tend to get in the way. Is this what that is? I'm too close to them?

Pulling back the chair next to mine inside the hospital Attending's Lounge table, Cassandra plops herself in it with a sigh. The chair protests the sudden weight, scraping against the tiled floor, and her afro quivers atop her head.

She peeks at me without moving her head. "Think she'll back out this time?" Watching her blowing on her coffee and chasing away the steam, I can tell she has the same sinking feeling as me.

My fingers drum against my hot cup, taking turns enduring the heat as I shrug, staring out the window that's drenched in raindrops. We're having a wet fall, and though I enjoy the rain, I can't help but miss the sun and the sliver of warmth it gives me, especially on days like today. There are times when it feels like the sun has the power to chase away the dark inside me.

Cassandra sits still—too still—as she studies me from the corner of her eye. She tries to remain inconspicuous with her perusal, and even though my attention isn't on her, I still notice her staring. With barely a sound, she lifts the remote from the center of the table and aims it at the TV hanging on the wall. Cassandra likes distractions.

Sound fills the room, a news anchor in mid-report. I continue to watch the rain, wishing I could be just like the drop that dribbles down the glass pane.

What would it be like to be the very thing that provides all life, sent from the heavens to a planet plagued with death? To know that I had a purpose as I floated from the glass before dropping to the soil. I'd be feeding life. I'd be the sustenance before returning to the heavens, repeating the cycle again and again. Life would be more predictable that way, more light-hearted and unplagued.

The news anchor's voice switches to a deeper, more urgent tone, and I'm pulled from my thoughts.

"The flu has arrived early this year. Mercy Memorial Hospital's free clinic has reported a widespread outbreak of fatigue, disorientation, and unexplained blood loss."

I glance at Cassandra, my brows furrowed as I continue to listen.

"They believe it to be a new strain of the virus and are urging the community to seek medical attention if you experience any of these symptoms."

Cassandra returns my frown before she mumbles, tracing the rim of her cup, "Have you heard anything about this?"

I shake my head. "No. Have you?"

"No." Her lips twist as she speculates. "What kind of virus produces unexplained blood loss?"

I turn my head back to the raindrops, my voice trailing off and my coffee left untouched. "I have no idea . . ."

CHAPTER FIVE

KATRIANE DUPONT

EARTH REALM

Taking the last step up the flight of stairs, I grasp the cheap handle and turn it, swinging open the door and accidentally forcing it open too wide. It bangs into the wall, and I jump a little at the sound. Cinnamon scented wax melts inside a warming pot, filling the space with a pleasant smell. I flick on the lights and begin peeling off my shoes. Tember's nostrils flare as she takes a big whiff, mentally assessing my living space. The T.V. is running, forgotten about in my haste to open the shop this morning. A news anchor is discussing some sort of medical emergency.

Symptoms are displayed across the screen in some sort of power-point presentation as the news anchor verbally lists them. Tember's attention instantly zones in on it, her eyes narrow until I break her concentration.

I swing my arm out, gesturing Tember to step farther inside. "Here we are. Home sweet home," I say a little too chipper. I clear my throat. I'm obviously nervous about having an angel live with me.

My apartment is small, just the way I like it. It has one bedroom and original hardwood floors. The living room is the first area we step into. Old, floral printed couches surround the small flat screen T.V. I found those couches on the side of the road a few years ago when I was renting this apartment out to a nice couple and not living in it myself. They were understanding when I needed the apartment back, and for that, I'm grateful.

A small kitchenette looks over the living room, an island with bar stools the only thing separating the two areas. Nothing in my apartment screams luxury. I'm a single woman running a business. Though I make a decent living, I don't see the point in granite countertops and fresh, handstitched leather couches. I make do with what I have, and I'm all the better for it.

Tember walks further into the apartment, her head slowly swiveling as she takes in the details. I can't tell if she's trying to discover the layout, critiquing the fact that this isn't a five-star hotel, or if she's scouting the area for danger. I roll my eyes anyway, her brash attitude rubbing my nerves raw.

"Make yourself at home," I mumble as she heads down the small hallway, stepping inside my bedroom. I shut the door, laying the keys on the small dining table. The table is never used, except for being the holder of all things postal.

I head to the kitchen, grab the kettle from the stove, and fill it with water. As I'm placing it back on the stove and turning the dial to heat the water, Tember pulls back a bar stool and seats herself at the island.

"Do you eat?" I ask, glancing over my shoulder before heading to the fridge.

"Yes," she answers like I should have known that already.

There isn't exactly a book out there stating all the details about every supernatural and otherworldly creature walking the realms. Though I wish there was, and it would be really handy, that'd be a huge liability. If it were placed in the wrong hands, it would have its own set of severe consequences with a big side of foreboding doom. Witches rely on legends told down through the generations. But, like a game of telephone, information can get lost or warped over time.

Bending in front of the fridge, I release a quiet sigh, falsely regretting the choice of letting her stay here. If I were being honest with myself, I'd admit that having someone else in my apartment sets my heart at ease. My fingers curl around the leftover lasagna inside a small, rectangular, cake pan-size, plastic Tupperware before I turn to face her. "Why are you so uptight?"

The perfectly sculpted eyebrows raise on her forehead. "I don't know what you mean."

My lips tense, and I walk to the microwave, placing the container inside. "Of course you don't. You're all business, aren't you?"

I wait for the microwave to beep, drumming my fingers on the counter and feeling her eyes drill a hole into the back of my head. My teeth clench together, grinding with the anxiety forming in the pit of my stomach.

Finally, she speaks, allowing me to release the breath I didn't know I was holding. "Why did you do it, Kat?"

Briefly closing my eyes, I resign myself to the fact that I'm going to have to tell her. I told myself I would never tell a soul about the incredibly stupid thing I did, but if she's going to stick around 'protecting me,' I might as well come clean. At this point, what could it hurt? She's already seen the second soul—the beast—I'm connected to.

"To save my coven," I mumble through my clenched teeth.

The microwave finishes its cycle at the same time the tea kettle whistles. I open the microwave, cooling its contents, while gathering the teabags, mugs, plates, and silverware.

Her pause in response causes my nervous energy to rise another level as I wait for her to berate me once more. "So, it was you who sacrificed to save the witches from the Red Death. How did you do it? How did you resurrect Myla?"

Turning to face her, surprise lights my features. She knows so much information and chose not to chastise me. Why?

I place her mug and plate on the counter and hand her a fork. She cuts a piece of steaming lasagna as I pull out a stool and gingerly sit beside her. "I summoned Erline. How do you know about the Red Death?" She pauses in lifting a bite to her mouth, one eyebrow raised. I roll my eyes. "Right. I'm your charge." My brows furrow as another thought hits me. "How did you know about the Red Death but not about me summoning Erline?"

Chewing her bite, she waits until she swallows before turning to face me. "Until recently, you weren't my only charge. Erma has," she pauses, considering her next words before continuing, "taken a special interest in you. I was allowed to come here, to walk with the humans, to watch over you."

I laugh without humor, waving my fork in the air. "Watch over me? I don't need watching over."

She takes another bite, this time not waiting to swallow before she answers, "You laugh, but I don't think you fully understand the situation you placed yourself in."

Lifting my mug to my lips, I take a scalding hot sip before placing it back on the counter. "Enlighten me then, oh wise one."

Her back straightens, and she shifts herself on the cushion of the stool, clearly unnerved by my attitude. "Your actions have had consequences. They always do. Allowing Erline to split your soul, replacing Myla as the second half—this will affect all of the realms like a ripple in the water."

Anger bubbles inside me, threatening to spill out of my mouth with a lash of impolite words. This isn't the first time I've heard this, and frankly, I'm getting sick of being told. Yet again, I'm being chastised for saving the witches. Yes, I share a soul with Myla's beast—with the First Born Witch. It would be great if everyone stopped reminding me.

"Your eyes are glowing," Tember says as a simple observation.

She lifts the last bite of her lasagna and stuffs it into her mouth, chewing with simplicity. She remains unaffected by me, and I don't know whether to take it as an insult or to be relieved that someone doesn't see me as a monster. My entire coven is frightened of me, assuming me more beast than witch. It's slightly relieving that someone isn't. Maybe I should be frightened of her . . .

Tember's eyes roam my small kitchenette before they land on mine. "I must say, it's nice to finally meet the legendary Myla." I shake my head, forcing Myla back inside me and the glow with it. She continues, "Legend has it, Myla wasn't only the First Born Witch. Our stories say she turned into a beast of fire at will. I'm curious. Is it Myla's beast inside you, or is it Myla herself?"

I fidget in my seat, my secret unfolding before me. Tember knows too much, and it makes me nervous. I'm sure she has good intentions; she is my angel after all. But I've worked too hard to keep this secret hidden—to keep all my secrets hidden. To have someone march into my life, knowing most of them, sets me on edge.

"Kat?" Tember calls, bending forward to capture my eyes with hers. "Which is it?"

I glare and lean slightly back. "Is it important to know?"

Her jaw clenches, the muscles rippling underneath her cheek. "Yes. If I am to protect you, I need to know the circumstance."

Sighing, my spine hits the backrest of the stool. "Her beast. Though, I've gained all of her powers." I gulp, a lie getting ready to pass through my mouth. "I'm in control here." I mentally chastise myself. *Only an idiot would lie to her angel.*

Tember searches my face, her expression blank. "You can try to fool yourself with words of dishonesty, but you can't fool me."

TEMBER

EARTH REALM

Nestled under her covers, Kat snores, the soft air passing through her nose before it mingles with the air. I stand in Kat's bedroom doorway, listening to it, mesmerized by it. Angels don't sleep, so naturally, I find it fascinating.

The blankets are tucked around her shoulders while she lays on her stomach. I can't see her face, but I imagine each muscle is relaxed instead of pinched with stress and lines of worry.

It's late. Most of this side of Earth's Realm is sleeping, placed inside their dreams by one of the many sandmen who cross over and roam this realm. Sandmen are not given the credit they deserve. Without them, each of these humans, and all those who partake in sleep, would be monsters in their own right. Sleep re-sets them. It is the very thing that rests their minds and works through their subconscious problems, all for a fresh start when they wake.

The sandmen cross over from the Dream Realm to this Realm, aiding the humans in this necessity. It won't be long now before one arrives.

Careful to remain noiseless, I cross my arms and lean against the door frame, my mind drifting to our earlier conversation. She has no idea how much danger she is in. Myla was a strong creation. Though loving and passionate, she was a force to be reckoned with. If she wanted something, she sought it out and grasped it in her fingertips.

If Erline brought her back, there must be a reason. Most Fee tend to not grant favors unless there is something in it for them. Though Myla is her daughter, I'd bet my wings that Erline has a second agenda. Only time—and evidence—will tell. I need that evidence.

A shimmer begins at the side of Kat's bed, a ripple in the air, distorting Kat's nightstand. I push my shoulder off the door frame, letting my hand drop to my side. A figure forms, a man dressed in burlap clothes long enough to reach his knees and wearing no pants. His skin is black, similar to the marble floors back on my realm. His pitch is so dark that I could have mistaken him for a shadow. I watch as he holds out his large palm. Tiny white grains gain in numbers, swirling on the surface like a small tornado before clearing, leaving behind a pile of white sand inside the dip of his palm. It sparkles without light, like the reflection light casts against a freshly fallen snow. He pinches the sand with his free hand, but before he can sprinkle it over my charge, I clear my throat.

White eyes that sparkle and match the sand inside his hand meet mine. I'm briefly startled by the lack of irises. I would assume he's blind, but as he holds my gaze, I come to the conclusion that he can clearly see. His fingers cover the sand, hiding it from my view as if I were here to steal it for myself.

A deep frown dips his barely visible eyebrows. I show my nature, my eyes illuminating a bright gold, causing the halo to form around my head.

"An angel," he mumbles, his voice deep with awe but his expression blank. His tenor is so low it's almost unintelligible, like the rumbling of a lion's purr.

I place my pointer finger over my lips, shushing him before he wakes Kat. Nodding my head toward the hallway behind me, I gesture for him to follow as I turn and leave Kat's room. My steps are confident as is my attitude. He will aide me in this small quest; that I am sure. I'm aware that it may not be of free will.

Once in the living room, I turn to wait for him, but instead, I'm briefly startled, rocking back on my heels before pulling my face back into a mask of security. He's right behind me, and I didn't even hear his advance. I've never met another creature so quiet.

"What do you want?" he rumbles. It takes me several moments to work through the deep-toned words.

"What do you know about her?" I nod my head toward the wall that shares her bedroom and the living room.

He glances at the wall before returning his white eyes back to me. "Kat or Myla?"

Double blinking, my head snaps to attention. "You know?" How did he know before I did? For the past few months, she's been my sole charge. I've kept a constant watch over her, and I didn't know until our conversation in her office. I must give her more credit. Kat has been extremely careful about hiding her secrets.

He inclines his head, briefly shutting his eyelids in affirmation. "A sandman knows everything about the dreamers he cares for."

Tilting my head, I consider this information. "How?"

"I know of her dreams. A sandman can see the dreams." His voice is emotionally lacking. Sandmen aren't built with emotions for a reason. Their Fee creator designed them this way so they'd never grow attached to their dreamers and would remain loyal to their Fee.

"Good." I nod once, fighting the urge to cross my arms. Sandmen frighten easily, and I need to remain impassive. "Who dreams? Myla or Kat?"

The sandman tilts his head to the side, considering me before answering, "Kat."

Relieved, my shoulders relax, and I blow out a breath. Myla hasn't taken over yet. With a little manipulation on my part, I can get answers on why she's here in the first place. "Can you guide a dreamer's dream?"

The sandman turns his head slightly to the left and twists his lips. It's as if he does not like my suggestion, like he's considering I may bring harm to his dreamer. I frown. That sort of emotion shouldn't be.

Before I can inquire about said emotion, he speaks. "Sandmen cannot grant fear-filled dreams. Those are not our doing."

Demons from the Demon Realm are the ones who manipulate the sandmen's work, creating all-consuming fear in a sleeping state to easily take their victims during their waking at a later time. Dreams are the easiest way to confuse a human—the quickest doorway. They groom their victims to weaken them.

I shake my head and cross my arms despite my previous resistance. "I don't want to strike fear in Kat or Myla." I take a careful step closer. "I want Myla's dreams to come to the forefront."

"What kind of dreams?" he asks, his eyelids narrowing and covering the sparkling white surface underneath. Again, I'm baffled by his ability to hold emotion. If I didn't know any better, I'd think this sandman has quite the protective instinct for Kat. This should be considered during later thoughts.

Rain begins to patter the window as the skies open like a drum roll for my oncoming words. "Memories." I smile, though it's anything but filled with glee. "Myla's memories."

AIDEN VANDER

EARTH REALM

The streets are quiet at this time of night as my sneakers pad against the sidewalk. My apartment isn't too far from the gym. The walk is a short one—it's the only thing that keeps me from buying a car. My home may be a pile of shit, but at least it's in walking distance to everything I need.

Off in the distance, a train wails a warning in crossing. There's only one train track I know of that still runs, and it passes through the forest outside the city, crossing under a bridge before it reaches the edge.

My foster family used to play there, and my foster father, Harold Tiller, still drives that train. Mr. and Mrs. Tiller are good people, but they could never love me as much their biological children. That train wails every night I walk home, and it's a constant reminder of the love I've never had.

Blankets of clouds crawl across the night sky, brightened by the lights of the city. I smell the oncoming rain and inhale it, calming my sour mood. My eyelids flutter as the aroma passes through my nose and swirls in the pit of my stomach. That one breath—that one inhale—relieves the weight pressing against my chest, and for just a moment, everything feels like it'll be okay.

A noise reaches my ears, a scuffle. I frown and quicken my pace, my 'hero' complex getting the better of me. I stop when I reach a certain area. Recognition hits me like the brick walls I stand next to. My dream . . . This is the place my dreams take me.

Taking pause and hesitation with my next step, my brain works frantically as I remember the swirls of unnatural, cold fog and the embrace of the motherly woman, Jane. My breath hitches when I feel pressure on my shoulder. It's comforting, warm. The smell of roses mixed with the oncoming rain.

The pressure tightens, and I feel each finger as they squeeze. I glance at my sweatshirt-covered shoulder and see nothing. No hand, fingers, or body belonging to the rose-scented woman. I blink, my eyelashes brushing my high cheekbone, and my muscles tense. *What the hell?* I feel her; I smell her. I know she's here. But I can't see her.

Slowly, I shift my head back in front of me and take a careful step forward. My inhales and exhales are exaggerated as my adrenaline pumps, replacing gripping curiosity with taunting slivers of fear.

A muffled cry for help bounces off the brick walls in the nearby alley before spilling into the street. The sound is just around the corner, and I can hear threats to a life being muttered with anger by a male voice.

I take another step, the pressure on my shoulder still there as the invisible hand urges me to remain calm.

My ankle joint cracks as I lift my foot and slowly place it on the cement, taking another step. A sprinkle of a cold raindrop hits the bridge of my nose before traveling to the crease of my nostril.

One more step. I turn my head in a surreal sort of way. Two men have a petite woman, about my age, pinned against the brick wall as they search her pockets and purse. Her skin is mahogany in color, a large afro circling around her head, and her coat barely covers her green scrubs, evidence that she's on her way home from a shift at the hospital. Her wild, wide eyes catch mine before the two men notice I'm even standing here.

Breath tickles my ear before soft words are spoken. "Save the girl," the voice of Jane speaks before the invisible hand squeezes my shoulder and releases the pressure, leaving me on my own.

So, she was here, right? I wasn't imagining that? I heard her clear as day, as clear as the thunder over my head. I felt her breath brush past my ear with each word. So . . . if she's here, or was here, but I couldn't see her, does . . . does that make her a ghost?

Snapping back to reality, I give a little shake of my head and fight the goosebumps freckling my skin. "Hey!" I yell at the men, anger and menace dipped in the word.

Their heads snap to me. Shock, like frightened deer discovering a set of headlights, crosses their faces before I take a step forward. I've seen the look before. Fear is an easy one to recognize in the boxing ring. It means one of two things: I'll win the fight, or my opponent is about to become irrational.

"Hey!" I shout again. A longer, wider step. Another raindrop hits my face. "Let her go."

The two men pause, considering, their eyes the size of saucers before they glance at each other, then back at me. *Shit. Irrational frightened deer.*

I quicken my pace as my broad frame lumbers in their direction. Their eyebrows dip as they narrow. Small, wicked smirks tilt their lips into false, minute smiles.

Gripping the brown leather purse from the first one's hands, I effectively yank it from his grasp before he pushes me into the brick wall. My shoulders hit with a thud, but my sweatshirt protects me against scraping the skin. The woman now forgotten, they advance on me, taking tactless, wide steps. I blow out a breath and momentarily hold it, centering myself and sharpening my senses.

Avoiding a punch, I duck, my sweatshirt snagging on the brick as my knees bend. His fist lands on the wall where the back of my head just was. He yanks it back with a grimace, cradling it with his other hand while hopping on his feet. He groans in pain but doesn't scream as I expected he would. That was a square punch—I wouldn't be surprised if he broke his hand.

I fling the purse to free my hands, and it lands with a thud at the woman's feet. I shove the man around the waist and he staggers from the force. Glancing at the woman, I shout for her to run, my arm flinging out in my desperation to snap her from her stupor. She breaks of her fear, blinking at me in rapid succession. I get a glimpse of her nametag dangling around her neck; Dr. Cassandra Grant it reads. She grabs her purse and takes off down the alley.

The other man hits me in the jaw, but my head doesn't move. There was no weight behind the punch. I grab the shoulder of his coat, striking his face three times before releasing him. My knuckles throb as his feet shuffle back. He holds his face, moaning, as bright red blood oozes between his cupped fingers.

I turn to face the other, and my foot stops mid-step, his sneer the only thing I see. Sudden, slicing discomfort the only thing I feel, hot, searing pain, spreads across my chest, and I frown, confused by the reason. A warm dribble tickles my skin under my sweatshirt, and I glance down in misunderstanding.

A handle pokes out of my chest, just above where my heart beats in a frantic rhythm. As I stare at the handle, a raindrop falls, splattering against the tiny black etches across its surface. It happens at such a slow pace, my head tilts to the side as I watch the single drop turn into dozens of tiny dots, scattering in every direction.

My heart beats again, constricted and forced, promising the end of life. I lift my head, the world moving in slow motion, and I look into the eyes of the blade's owner. His sneer fades, his eyebrows raising high into his forehead. He stares at the knife with wide eyes, then at his hand, then returns them back to mine.

The strength leaves my legs, and I drop to my knees, clutching the handle of the knife. Blood seeps from the wound, spilling onto the crook of my thumb and pointer finger. It's hot, warming the chill of the skin on my hand. My chest is slippery, my sweatshirt soaked with thick, red moisture, and the pain blooms to regions of my body I didn't know existed. It's as if it crosses through every nerve, like throbbing electricity.

The other man curses and comes into my line of sight. I breathe, the sound loud to my ears, the pain all-consuming, the chill of my skin frightening. The other man rakes a hand through his hair before shoving his shock-still friend—whose hand is still mid-air, suspended out in front of him.

I blink, slow, exaggerated, time standing still. Thudding against the concrete, it takes a moment to realize I've fallen to my side, just as the purse did a minute ago. My hand jostles the knife, sending it a little deeper into the wound, into my heart. I feel a pop come from within my chest, the pain searing deep within before spreading to the surface, stealing my breath away.

The men hesitate, shifting their weight from side to side. "Take his shoes," one squeaks.

Frightened, irrational deer, I briefly think.

My feet are yanked before the chill of the air licks their soles, my shoes now in the hands of their new owner. I hear the patter of their feet as they take off down the alley.

My mouth hangs open, and I suck in air, desperate for more time, for this to not be real. I blink, hear the silent pop as my eyelids separate from each other. I hold them open too long and tears begin to form across their surface, spilling out of the outer edge of my eyelids.

A transparent figure steps into my line of sight, and my gaze shifts to it. Her eyes hold such grief, such sadness, as tears stream down her slightly-aged cheeks. *Jane*, my slow brain provides me.

She bends to her knees, placing them on the cement. "It's almost over," she whispers, brushing the back of her hand against my cold cheek. She places the other over my fingers, holding the handle of the knife with me.

Shushing in soothing whistles, her sounds of comfort mingle with the raindrops as they pick up their pace, splatting against the pavement, against my exposed face.

My body shivers, and my muscles tense from the lack of blood as it drips from my wound, down my side, and seeps through my sweatshirt onto the concrete. Muscles cramp, begging for the very thing they need to keep them alive. I grow weak, the effort to breathe becoming a tedious task, and I watch Jane blink again, another tear mixing with the moisture.

"That's it," she comforts. "You're almost there."

I'm dying. Is this what it feels like?

I breathe, slow, leisurely, my life flashing before my eyes. A motherless boy. A life in a foster home. A young man on his first date—his first kiss. The joy of buying my first car. The feeling of freedom as I stepped foot inside my first apartment. The echo inside the gym. Feeling my muscles burn with each step in a jog. The smell of the trees as I ran. A pat on the back—a job well done—and the feeling of joy as I held up a trophy when I won my first boxing match.

"Shh," she soothes, another stroke against my cheek. My eyelids flutter, my heart stops, and then I'm weightless. I feel nothing—pain or emotion—except an empty freedom. The breath leaves my lungs, working its way past my tongue in a sluggish, effortless slither.

CHAPTER SIX

KATRIANE DUPONT

MYLA'S MEMORY

Where the hell am I?

I glance around, my brows furrowed and my heart racing. I'm confused about why I'm here. Where is here, exactly?

Houses that look freshly built, but poorly so, scatter in a circle around a large open area. They aren't painted and look as though they wouldn't withstand a gust of wind, let alone a strong storm. The houses are adorned with nothing—no lawn decorations, no shrubs. Smoke exits their chimneys, mixing with the air before dissipating, but not before the smell of burning wood tickles my nose. I twitch my nostrils and squeeze my eyes shut. It wouldn't do to sneeze.

The women are dressed in long dresses with square necklines; the bombard sleeves accent the arms of the multi- and pastel-colored outfits. Some women have white linen coifs placed over their heads, similar to a veil, while others have more of a bonnet-styled hood. I blink slowly, one side of my face pinching in confusion and disbelief.

The men are dressed in layers, and their accessories are quite feminine. I almost giggle. Feathers adorn their hats, fur hangs from their shoulders, and the colors of their clothing are rich and vibrant. They're dressed more luxuriously than the women, a complete contradiction to my era.

Their first layer looks like a long dress with a rope wrapped around the waist several times before it's tied in the front. Capes hang from their backs, billowing out behind them. The cloth around the shoulders is puffy, and the stockings around their legs are snug.

Where the heck am I?

These people, this place, is foreign to my time. I watch, my head swiveling from side to side and my facial features wide with shock. The people roam dirt paths and unkempt lawns, some seeming to be out and about just to chat.

A few citizens are arm in arm, talking in French as they go about their day. A man off in the distance is chopping wood, the sound jarring my eardrums each time the ax connects and splits the wood. A gaggle of women gossip off in the distance, laughing with each other while they wash their clothes inside a large barrel of water.

It's a cool day. Fallen leaves are scattered haphazardly. A breeze picks up, creating a circular leaf tornado that travels a short distance before they fall back to the ground. Each time a person takes a step, the crunch of leaves under their feet draws my attention.

I'm in another time, another place, like I've been brought back to when civilization and towns were just discovered.

My eyes pause when they reach the center of the houses. Gallows are placed, and three thick-roped nooses dangle from wooden posts. Short cages rest under the gallows, the bars made poorly of iron to keep their prisoners captive. It's as if they placed it there as a warning for wrong-doers—the center of attention, a constant reminder to obey the law.

As the townspeople roam about, they pass right by me, as if I'm not even there. I twirl around, getting a better view of my situation, and just as I face the opposite direction, a couple passes right through me. I gasp, slightly bent over and clenching my stomach, before frowning and glancing back at them over my shoulder. They continue as if I weren't here.

Bloody hell.

A horse whinnies, and I look in the direction of the sound. A stable is placed behind the circle of houses. Behind that, a stream flows, just visible through the thinning tree line.

"Myla, my love," a man greets in loving French words. I whip my head around, recognizing the language and the name.

My ancestral magic is French; French being my first language, English my second. The coven teaches their young witch-lings French first so we're able to control and understand our magic as it comes.

I eye Myla, my eyes narrowed and skeptical, recognizing her name for what it is—The First Born Witch. Is this really her? Or is the name a coincidence?

Dressed in the ridiculous outfit every other man wears here, a brown-haired guy takes the steps needed to fold a slender blond woman in a hug. Myla smiles at him, tilting her cheek as he places a hesitant kiss on it. She's beautiful, and as they turn together to watch the two twin girls playing in the grass, I catch his profile.

A strong jaw, full, wide lips, and chocolate brown eyes bring together his charming features. He's devilishly handsome. By looks, he's certainly a catch, but I can see the mischief swirling within his eyes. He's untrustworthy—that is very clear.

He wraps his arm around her and she leans into his chest. "Where have you been, Corbin?" she mumbles. Her voice is so full of distrust that I dip my chin in confusion. Love is the language of her actions, but her tone utters revulsion.

His lips barely move as he replies, "You surely already know."

Myla's scoff is quiet, but I hear the anger behind her next words. "The Demon Realm can't run itself?"

I double blink, taking a step closer to hear the conversation better. Her eyelids narrow, a glare taking over her beautiful blue eyes while the smile remains on her lips. I glance around, watching as other couples stare at them with envy as they walk by. They must be this town's role model couple. Is that why they pretend to love one another? To put on a show? And for what? Are they a powerful couple?

He places a kiss on her forehead, his lips lingering longer than they should. "You know it can't."

"You promised me . . ." She pulls back, looking into his eyes with a sneer lifting her top lip. "You promised that if I married you, you'd leave your Fee duties behind."

Fee duties . . . the Demon Realm . . . Is this . . .? No, it can't be. Is he Corbin, Fee of the Demon Realm? The breath hitches in my chest. I remember his reputation in the legends of our lessons. He's a trickster, a charmer—his sole purpose and goals are strictly for himself.

The little girls giggle, and my gaze switches back to them. Before my vision can focus on their figures, the dream transforms.

I'm inside a house, the living room lit by candles placed throughout. A fire burns in the pit, warming the space and the two girls with its flames as it consumes the wood inside it. The little girls have dolls placed between them, red yarn for a few strands of hair. They giggle as they hop their dolls about the floor, a little game of pretend that causes me to smile. They're so innocent, so adorable, with no care or worry in the world.

Behind me, I hear voices muttered, the tone thick with anger. I look at the girls once more before seeking out the voices.

There, in the kitchen, stands Myla—her hands clenched at her sides, dressed in an old-fashioned nightgown that reaches the floor. A spell book is open on the table while she glares at Erline. It's hard for me to look at anything but Erline—her presence seems to take up the entire space even if she's a small, slender woman. She's exactly as I remember her. Her long blond hair reaches her knees, matching the flow of her dress that ripples even without a twitch of wind.

"He hasn't been back for two months, Mother. It's time to fake his death. You know how humans can get. They're already suspicious. It's as we feared—the witch trials are going to begin. If they think anything untoward is going on—" Myla blows out a breath, fanning the strand of hair dangling in front of her face.

Erline folds her hands in front of her, patience wearing thin. "My darling. You know how different the times are in each realm. He's a Fee in charge of boisterous demons. Something is surely occupying his time. Be patient."

Myla slams her fist on the table. "He's never been gone this long. He's abandoned us. Abandoned me." She paces the small quarters of the kitchen, her fingers shaking at her sides. "I should have never listened to you. I should have married Joseph."

"My daughter would never have married a stable boy!" Erline shouts, unclasping her hands and slamming one on the wooden table. She takes a deep breath, working to calm herself as the flames from the candles quiver. She forces herself to keep her tone soft, dipping her chin just so as if that would help pinch her voice to a quieter tone. "This was an arranged marriage for a reason, Myla. He was promised to you by your father before you were born. It was out of my hands. Someone as strong as yourself can't marry a simple human." Erline straightens her dress. "I will travel to the Demon Realm and see what's holding your lover's attention. This discussion is over. You will wait until I return to take any further action. Do not be a fool."

Without waiting for a response, she conjures wind inside the tiny space. It swirls around her, the flames of the candles left untouched but Myla's hair whips about. As the winds pick up speed around Erline, she disappears, fading inside it.

Myla releases a frustrated growl. Magic sparks crackle in the air, so thick I can taste it against the buds along my tongue, and the flames flare before flicking out of life, sending the kitchen into darkness.

She stalks from the room, but I remain where I'm at, confusion clogging my thoughts as my eyes flick about the room with aimless abandon. I pause at the tiny window, a figure catching my attention.

Outside the window is a set of eyes, the expression on the face of the eyes' owner is wide and wrinkled with stress. Long hair covers half his face, smudged with soot. Dumbstruck *and full of fear, I watch as the peeper shakes his head in quick motions and runs from the window, fear driving his purpose.*

AIDEN VANDER

EARTH REALM

I float into the air, Jane watching as some sort of invisible force lifts me. I'm transparent just like she is. A ghost. A shell of my once life. Dead. A shade floating along the Earth.

My stomach heaves as my feet settle to the concrete behind Jane, seeing my bleeding body against the ground, my lifeless, unseeing eyes wide open. The skin around my face is relaxed—my body no longer looks like it's me.

The clouds open, rain dropping sheets in a heavy flow, passing through me as if I'm not standing here. Have I ceased to exist? Or could it be possible there is something more for me on the other side?

I hold my arm out, watching the beads of liquid pass through. My eyes move to the concrete, a red river streaming past my shell of a body. I watch it for a moment, fascinated that one body could hold so much liquid. And yet, that liquid is the only thing that kept me alive. Now, it trickles like a creek down the slopes of rock, searching for a new place to call home.

Jane stands, slowly at first, before she takes careful, considering steps in my direction. "Aiden?" My eyes flick to hers but my head remains downcast. "Ready?" she asks, her hand held out for me to grasp.

Glancing once more at the river of red, I take her hand in mine. We walk down the alley and vanish as sirens wail in the distance.

Help is coming. Help is too late.

ELIZA PLAATS

EARTH REALM

My feet slap against the wet pavement. The hospital parking lot is nearly empty; most of the employees have long since left. The glowing hospital sign behind me lights my way, shining the beaded raindrops across the surface of my car.

Fumbling inside my purse, I silently curse as I shove the objects inside about before my fingers touch the tip of jagged metal—my keys. A shout behind me draws my attention, and I whirl around off kilter.

"Dr. Plaats?" a nurse calls. Her long brown ponytail weaves from side to side, and her tennis shoes smack against the wet cement as she runs to me, like the slapping of naked skin. "There's an incoming trauma." She huffs out the air from her short sprint. "Surgical."

As the on-call doctor for the night, it's my job to see to the E.R. My bones ache, and my muscles quiver from exhaustion, but adrenaline consumes my blood pumping through each vein. I had just finished with the last incoming trauma, checking on the patient in the recovery wing before I left for the night. It would seem sleep won't come as soon as I'd hoped.

Being a doctor can have the greatest reward or the lowest. Either way, it doesn't stop my adrenal glands from releasing this addictive hormone through my body. It's the fight or flight response. I choose to fight. I choose to save a life. I choose my addiction.

Dropping my keys back inside, I throw my purse back over my shoulder and jog with her to the sliding doors of the E.R. entrance. They open just as the ambulance pulls into the cul-de-sac, its sirens wailing and the cubed lights flashing on the roof. My heart races, excitement and slight fear forming in my chest. A few more faceless nurses exit the building. One grabs my purse and fits me with gloves and a yellow plastic trauma gown.

As we reach the back of the ambulance, the driver, dressed in the standard issue white button-down shirt and black slacks, opens the back, giving me the full report. "Patient's name is Aiden Vander. Age thirty-one. Stab wound to the chest. He's been unresponsive since we arrived on the scene." The driver glances at me, sorrow pinching his eyes.

Thirty-one—such a young age to die, but it's my job to try and bring back the life. It's a challenge I'm willing to take, or at least try.

The response team wheels the patient from the back of the ambulance to the ground after lowering the wheels. "We haven't been able to get a heartbeat."

I nod to him. "Well, seeing as the knife is poking out of his chest where his heart is, I'd guess that's the cause of the problem," I mumble in full sarcasm.

The ambulance driver snarls, his nerves already raw. "There's no need to get snippy, doctor."

We rush inside. The wheels squeak in tune with the sliding glass doors until we are bathed in warmth from inside the building. The team and I rush to the first examination room available, a nurse already there flipping on the lights and machines.

I glance at the victim, tilting my head to the side to get the full profile, while someone ties my gown around my back. A matte black handle pokes out of his chest, and his skin and shirt is covered in blood and rain. Surrounding the entrance of the knife, a few strands of his hooded sweatshirt are frayed. Blood dribbles from the side of his lips, the edges of the red droplets dried at the square point of his jaw. He's handsome and young. Surely, he has loved ones depending on his survival. At this point, however, it would take a miracle.

A nurse connects the heart monitor while another hands me the paddles. I glance at the monitor showing no heartbeat, and my heart drops to the floor in fear. This knife has claimed its victim. No amount of medical practice will save this man.

CHAPTER SEVEN

ELIZA PLAATS

EARTH REALM

"Is there family?" I ask the nurse. Her fingers click against the keyboard as she records the time of death. Her attitude is detached as if this is an everyday occurrence. I suppose it is for her. I don't often work in the E.R., but she does.

Her fingers pause their march, and her head swivels toward me. "No family. The police had already checked. There's a guy from his gym though."

Death doesn't scare me anymore. I stare at this man, a man the same age as me, and I see a shell. It's a shell that once held a soul, a being, and now . . . nothing. Death is unpredictable. It's a fear everyone should have. He could have had a life, one worth living. Instead, his prize for trying to live, before he could really *live*, is death.

Guilt rides me like a horse. Is there more I could have done? If he had arrived minutes earlier, could I have saved him?

Blame starts forming in my thoughts where it shouldn't. This is nobody's fault but the person who put that knife there in the first place. People are wicked—nobody deserves to have their life taken from them. The only thing keeping me from slipping over the edge is that possibly, just possibly, he's in a better place.

I place my hand over his, my small fingers giving condolences for the life lost, in hopes that he can see me somewhere, showing him affection in the best way I know how. This man died alone and quite possibly scared. The least I can do is show his spirit compassion.

He's a large man, and even through his blood-soaked sweatshirt, I can see he took good care of his body and health. For the life of me, I can't fathom why he has no one. Was he too consumed with his career? Did he simply choose this life? I'll never know. His future is now gone from him. A lump forms in my throat—it's never easy to lose a life, especially if that life was under the care of my capable and well-trained hands.

Removing my hand, I walk to the edge of the bed, unfolding the white blanket that lies there. Carefully, I spread the sheet over him, and just before I cover his face, I steal one more glance.

"You heading out?" the nurse asks, breaking me from this trance.

"Yeah," I mumble while smoothing out the wrinkles from the blanket.

She shifts her body to me, the wheels on the stool protesting the movement. "Good. Get some rest, Dr. Plaats."

Nodding, I stretch my neck, and without a backward glance, I exit the room. My purse lay on the nurses' station counter, and I wrap my fingers around the handle. My emotions are raw and exposed, and my conscience desperately tries to block the emotional pain. This isn't my first encounter with death, and sadly, I know it won't be my last.

Placing one foot in front of the other, I head further away from the E.R., back to home with the intent of sleep.

Tomorrow will be better, I promise myself.

KATRIANE DUPONT

EARTH REALM

Just beyond Myla's living room window, I am standing outside the home taking in the scene before me. My brain feels like it has a case of whiplash, and every muscle I have is tense with fear.

The city is in chaos; people are screaming and running in aimless, haphazard actions as they seek shelter from the threat

112

that plagues their town. Vampires rush to their next victim,
throwing them against trees, against homes, until the human
lays lifeless. Blood, debris, even limbs, scatter the night's
ground.

A scream erupts just behind me, and I swivel, watching a
vampire pierce the neck of a helpless man, blood soaking the
fur-hemmed cape along his shoulders. He struggles against the
vampire, attempting to dislodge his teeth, but it's too late—his
movements slow, and the life leaves his eyes.

My breath comes fast, my heart pumping so hard that
I'm sure the vampires would hear it if I were actually here.

Voices come from inside Myla's home, and I turn back to
the window with a jerky twirl. Myla is kneeling next to her twins,
speaking to them in a soft but rushed tone. "Stay here," she
says. "Don't open the doors. Don't let anyone inside. Do you
understand?"

Their tiny blond heads bobble as they clutch their dollies
for comfort. Myla nods, satisfied that they understand, and
rushes toward the front door. She swings it open, and it bangs
against the wall inside; she steps through and closes it before
she's noticed.

A vampire approaches her, but she raises her hand,
fingers curled like cuffs. The vampire is lifted into the air, his feet
dangling, and blood-tinged spittle squirts from his mouth as he
hisses at her.

Myla sneers in return, a frightening menace dipping her
eyebrows and lifting her top lip to expose her teeth. She lifts her

other hand, making a grabbing motion before yanking her arm back. The vampire shrieks before his heart is ripped from his chest. The black organ drops to the grass with a thud.

I watch the slick heart, my brain refusing to comprehend what I've just witnessed. The vampire's ash falls to the grass next to it before the heart itself turns to the same glittering black dust.

Myla continues to stand next to her door like a guard dog, surely to protect her children. Where is Corbin? Why isn't he here protecting her? And Erline?

Hearing the shriek of their now dead vampire brother, the remaining vampires whip their heads in Myla's direction, blood red eyes set on her figure. They hone in on the new threat. Or perhaps . . . perhaps this is the reason they're here. Why else would they choose this village? What does it hold for them?

Maybe there's no such thing as a coincidence. After all, vampires were set about the Earth to find Myla in the first place. Could this be a simple vampire feeding? I think not.

Low hisses and guttural rumbles spill past their dripping fangs. The unnatural sound fills the night air, easily surpassing the screams of pain, and raises goosebumps across my arms. They charge from all directions, their speed legendary, almost a blur. My hand flies to my chest. Is this how she died? "Myla!" I scream in warning even though I know I won't be heard.

As her name rips through my throat, it's cut short, my eyes not believing what they're seeing. Her skin quivers and ripples beneath the surface. A cloud of smoke spills from her

114

nostrils like a fog machine on Halloween night. Her eyes glow the brightest of neon orange, and black, glimmering scales begin to slice through her skin from the inside out. It looks excruciating, but she gives no indication of the pain. She grows, her body completely transformed into a beast of legends, until she's as tall as her house.

"A dragon," I breathe through clenched teeth. I knew she was a dragon. After all, this is the form of Myla that Erline had resurrected and inserted inside me. But the shock of seeing it first-hand . . .

She stands on all fours in magnified glory. I marvel at her. Each muscle twitches and flexes, a testament to her strength. Every movement she makes, no matter how minor, causes a wave, a ripple, under her scales.

Her black wings look like they belong to an overgrown bat. They're leathery but sleek, and her scales shine so bright in the moonlight that they almost look wet. Spikes, like the fins along the spine of a fish, web throughout her back and head. Rows of sharp razor teeth chomp, saliva stringing from the top teeth to the bottom, as she opens her muzzle before shaking her head. The spikes wave as her head does and the muscles contract and expand along her shoulder as she picks up a large claw and smashes a vampire. I double blink, the vampire now a pile of ash. She crushed it like it was nothing but one of the many leaves scattered about the grass—as if the vampire wasn't made of bones and rotting flesh.

The roar that escapes Myla's mouth is deafening, and I cover my ears with a cringe. Her muscles shake with the effort to *produce it, each scale waving like the ocean as her neck expands. Her spiked tail whips to the side, and she draws in a breath, her rib cage increasing in size and glowing with billowing fire from within. She releases the breath, and a stream of flames spout from her mouth, aimed directly at the shocked vampires.*

The heat is excruciating. I can feel it licking my skin and flattening my goosebumps. I back up several feet, almost bumping into the side of the house to escape it.

Myla's dragon roars again before I have a chance to recover from the first one. The sound mixes with the screams of her victims, echoing off each house. My heart pounds, fear wracking my body causing me to quiver.

This beast seems untamable, bent on destruction. I briefly wonder if Myla has control here, or if the beast is the one in the driver's seat. For the first time, I fear the dragon and the power it holds. What if I can't control it? What if it destroys everything, like my mother said it might?

Before I can cover my ears, it fades, the dream transforming once more.

My heart pounds, refusing to back down from its fear. I struggle with wanting to run, to hide, even though I stand in the corner of the gallows' prison cells.

Moonlight filters in through the cracks in the wood floor above. The roped nooses dangle in a slight breeze. Ruckus and shouts erupt into the night as chanting, "Kill the witch," is repeated. I peek between the poorly built bars, the citizens gathered in the town's center behind me.

I ignore them and instead, turn my attention back to Myla, watching her pace the dirt inside the cell. I'm leery of her, untrusting of the beast she is. How did she transform back? Did she kill every vampire? Did the dragon kill any innocents?

She fidgets with the cuffs of her dress, busying her fingers. Her eyes flick about in fear, matching my own. Does she fear the humans as much I fear her right now? She's a dragon— why isn't she breaking out of this prison? Death will surely follow her. There's no way every citizen didn't witness her second form.

Hands slam into the bar beside me, fingers wrapping around the iron, and I jump, my nerves raw. My hand flies to my heart, and a tiny squeak escapes my lips.

Corbin's eyes peer through the bars. The flame covered torches held by people behind him light his dark hair but hide his facial features. "Myla," he whispers. "Myla, what did you do?"

She turns to face him, her eyes wide and glossy with unshed tears. "They saw me. They saw me.*"*

He blinks, his mouth flapping open and shut, words escaping him. "How?" he growls.

Myla wipes a tear with rough, trembling fingers. "A nest of vampires found me." She spits the words with raw hatred. "They were attacking the town. Was I to watch everyone die?" Her foot lifts from the ground, and she paces once more. Puffs of dry dirt mingle in the open space of the cell, clouding my vision as she stomps.

"Yes," he snarls. "You were to let them die. They're humans. What of our girls?"

She lifts her head for a moment, meeting his eyes. "They're safe. Mother has them."

Corbin blows out a relieved sigh, tilting his head toward the ground and resting it against the bars. "I'll free you. We just need a distraction."

She stops, her hand flying to her chest, and her fingers begin fidgeting with the hem of her square neckline. Tears spill down her cheeks and she sniffles. "No. I can't."

He looks up at her through his eyelashes. "Why?"

"You can't expose yourself."

Corbin's fist slams against the bars. "Myla, see reason. You can't escape this marriage by death. You're mine."

She pauses in her words, lowering her voice as the citizens begin approaching. Taking a few steps forward she says, "By death do us part, remember?"

Waving her hand in the air, he shimmers before disappearing in a roar of rage. The townspeople, close enough to witness her magic, scream in fright.

****

My chin is placed in my hand as I rest my elbow against the streak-free counter. The rain continues, leaving perfect oval drops against my shop's window before gravity slides them to the ground. At least it's more of a drizzle instead of yesterday's torrential and sporadic downpour.

Tember is in the breakroom, attempting to make coffee. I hear her mumbling angry words and slamming the coffee pot into the machine. My breath heaves as I sigh, continuing to stare out the window.

I feel like I haven't slept. Like all I did last night was watch a movie behind closed eyelids. Myla has been quiet, barely stirring or commenting as she normally does.

Tember settled in quickly after borrowing some of my clothes. I woke to find her hand in a box of cereal, munching away on the stool. This is going to take some getting used to. After months of being on my own, having another person around has its benefits, but it also has its drawbacks. One of us is going to have to pick up more food. Since she isn't from this realm and has probably never been inside a grocery store, that chore will fall on my shoulders.

I smile as a thought crosses my mind. Maybe I'll take her with so that next time she eats all the food, I can send her to the store instead.

My smile fades as flashes of the dreams surface once more. They were unsettling . . . still are, actually. Myla's memories hold so many secrets and deceit. I'm left with so many questions, questions that I can surely ask her now, but the truth is, I'm terrified to know the answers.

I witnessed her power—both her magic and her dragon. She sent a Fee back to his realm and effortlessly burned vampires until they were nothing but ash. Even then, I don't know anyone who can challenge a Fee in such a manner, spouse or not. Her power terrifies me on such a level that I'm rethinking of ever tapping into it, of ever making that deal in the first place. My mother was right—she could be my undoing.

Her daughters, the little blond girls who played on the floor, their frightened faces as their mother protected them, those two girls are my ancestors. They're the beginning of a long line of witches, birthed by the First Born and Fee of the Demon Realm, granddaughters to Kheelan and Erline. What happened to them? How could this knowledge be lost to us?

It begs to reason that Erline kept this a secret. The girls were too young to know who or what their father was. Erline would keep this information hidden, holding the children close to her heart for protection, right?

The thought of having three different Fee bloodlines running through my system is mind-boggling. I feel used and betrayed to have this knowledge lost to us, like half my ancestral history was a lie. Who did the girls think their father was? What did Erline tell them?

I grit my teeth. Not only am I the great, great, so-on-and-so-forth granddaughter of Kheelan, I'm also the same to Corbin. The tales we learned as children are anything but the full truth. What would my coven do when they knew most of our history was completely false? Would they continue to hold Erline as a beloved creator? Or would they demand answers like I'm tempted to?

Thinking about that for a moment, I make a choice. I can't tell them even if they would spare me a minute to listen. It's always a good plan to know the entire truth before I spill what I've learned. I just hope I'm given the chance to find out.

Scanning the windows once more for a distraction of any kind, my mind continues to wander until my eyes stop in their tracks, focusing on the figure leaning against the brick wall across the street.

He's coatless, and his shirt is soaked from the rain. His thumbs rest inside his pockets. Raindrops drip from his brown hair before they splash to the ground.

I watch him, my head tilting to the side. He seems oddly out of place, but he glances around like a tourist enjoying the city on a bright summer day. He doesn't shiver from the rain or his soaked clothes, and he seems as though he has no other place to be, besides leaning against a brick wall.

My frown is replaced with shock when his head slowly turns my direction. His eyes latch onto mine, and my breath hitches in my throat. "Corbin," I whisper as I take a few steps back, bumping into a box laying on the floor behind the counter.

Corbin's head shifts slightly to the right as he considers me, as if he heard me, and his eyebrows pinch together slightly. My feet stop in their tracks, and I feel compelled to go to him, to reach out and unfurrow those brows. Why is he here? How did he find me? Does he know who I am?

No, she shouts in my head, taking over my feet and planting them to the ground.

We stare at each other, my breaths slow and even but loud to my own ears as I drink him in. I'm briefly disgusted by my own actions—by having desires for a distant grandfather.

Corbin shifts his feet, breaking the eye contact and looking back to the ground. The lines on his forehead furrow.

He tilts one more time, a considerate expression, until a bus blocks my view from him as it travels along the road, cascading water droplets in fine sheets. The bus moves at a quick rate, and by the time it's gone from my window, so is Corbin.

Tember walks up behind me. "You should consider an easier contraption to make coffee." She places a mug on the counter. Taking a look at my confused expression, she follows my line of sight out the window. "What is it?"

I take a moment, collecting my thoughts about what this could possibly mean before shaking my head. "There was a guy standing there." I point. "And he just disappeared."

She walks to the window and peers down the sidewalks. "Do you know him?"

My eyebrows knit, and I glance at my mug, not seeing it. "Corbin," I mumble.

Her body freezes, and her shoulders bunch before she turns in slow motion on the ball of her heel.

"Corbin," she says, exaggerating each letter. "Fee of the Demon Realm, Corbin?" I nod. "Do you know him?"

"I just know of him and that he was married to Myla."

She frowns, her eyebrows pinching together. "What are you talking about?"

I sigh. I was hoping to keep this information to myself until I could work out the purpose of it. If she's here for my protection, and Corbin is lurking about, it's best to at least tell her a little of what I now know. "Myla is showing me her memories while I sleep. She and Corbin lived in France in the 1600s. They were married with two daughters."

Tember scoffs though it feels forced. I know Angels aren't one hundred percent honest and forthcoming—it seems like nobody is these days. I'd be interested in learning what she already knows, but I should make it a point to keep my distance.

She scratches her cheek. "That's not what the legends say."

I narrow my eyes, suspicious of what she's not telling me. "No. No, it's not. I think it's time I have a chat with Erline."

Tember chews on the inside of her lip, a rare show of anxiety. "How did Corbin find you?"

I shrug while lowering my index finger and touching the tip of the rim on my mug, curiosity fueling my purpose. I watch the steam continue to rise from the brew, and before it has a chance to evaporate, I cup it in my hands like a child capturing a fly.

Bringing my cupped hands to my mouth, I blow inside, through the small space between my thumbs. Tember is silent as she watches with interest, her head tilting slightly to the side.

Slowly, I open my hands like a flowering rosebud in the wake of the sun. There, between my two palms, the steam plays with streams of fire, swirling around each other in a game of twister, making the shape of a ball. My eyes grow wide with wonder, and I bend eye level with it.

Tember walks the few feet to me, peering at the contents in my hand. She sticks her hand out and touches the ball. I frown. I know the flames won't hurt me—every time I touch something hot, it feels no different than touching something cold. I can feel heat, and I know the pain should be there, but it never mars my skin or leaves blisters when it should. However, shouldn't the heat hurt her?

"Doesn't that hurt?" I ask after a moment of watching her in fascination.

She shakes her head, her brown curls shaking like ribbons. "We don't feel pain." Tilting her head to the side, she mumbles her thoughts aloud, "Water. Air. Fire . . ." She glances around the counters.

"What?" I ask, my voice approaching hysterical giggles. It's too much—too much for one day. The memories, Corbin—it's causing a miniature breakdown inside me, and I can feel myself losing it. Add to that the constant discoveries of Myla's magic and what I can do with it, and it just intensifies this festering ache inside the pit of my stomach.

Nodding to the swirling ball in my hand, she supplies me with the reasoning for her thoughts. "Steam is water and air. The flames—fire." She steps back, glancing at the floor before her eyebrows unfurrow and a small grin replaces her downturned lips.

I feel Myla stir inside me like she's privy to what Tember's about to do.

Tember bends, picking up a tiny stone from the floor between pinched fingers, and faster than I thought possible, she stands. I double blink at her speed, used to her moving at the pace of humans. Perhaps she does that on purpose. Perhaps she's been trying not to scare me. Once again, I feel like I'm being treated like a child. However, at this very moment, I almost wish I was one. Maybe then the weight of so many things wouldn't be resting on my tiny, insignificant shoulders.

"Earth," she says. She glances at the barely visible stone before her eyes shift to the ball swirling in my hands. Looking at the door, she takes the few steps to it before turning the "open" sign to "closed." Her gait is purposeful as she heads back toward me.

"Come," she demands. I frown but do as she asks.

Leaving the counter, I walk around the edge, careful to avoid the boxes I just bumped into moments before, and follow her back into my office. She holds the door open for me, the stone still trapped in her fingers, before closing it with a soft click. I stand there, waiting to see what she does next, the ball still in my hands.

"Ready?" she asks.

I clear my throat and shift my weight. "Sure."

Her eyebrows dip a fraction with concentration, or perhaps concern, and she reaches her hand forward, dropping the stone inside the swirling ball of water, fire, and air.

As soon as the stone hits, it dives straight to the center, hovering there, floating and turning in a circle on its own. For a moment, nothing happens, and I'm relieved. That is until the ball crackles and grows, seizing the oxygen in my lungs. My head juts back in surprise. I'm pissed that I allowed her to talk me into this with such ease, without knowing what we were doing or the consequences that may follow.

The ball leaves my palms, traveling at a slow pace to hover just before my altar table. It continues its size adjustment, flattening itself into the shape of a large sphere doorway taller than myself. The contents swirl inside, the fire most dominant, like a vortex. A slight continuous rumble echoes as a distant thunder comes from the doorway.

"What the hell?" I ask, taking a step forward.

A portal, Myla provides me, her voice dipped in anger. If she didn't want us to do this, why didn't she stop me like she did when I attempted to go to Corbin?

For the first time, I speak to her, "Why didn't you use this to escape the gallows?"

Tember glances at me, concern crossing her eyebrows. "What?"

I ignore her, waiting for an answer Myla doesn't return.

"Who are you talking to?" Tember asks, stepping forward.

I glance at her but keep my mouth shut in a fine line. She blinks twice before looking at the swirling flat sphere in front of us. "Not hell," she mumbles. "A portal."

She looks back at me. "You have the ability to manipulate all of Earth's elements to walk between the realms."

I close my eyes. "It's not my magic. It's Myla's."

She laughs, her head tilting back so her face is level with the ceiling. It startles me for a moment, and I wonder if she's losing her mind just as I feel like I am.

Tember rarely shows emotions. After her fit of humorless giggles, she looks back at me. "You may be two different people," she explains as she cocks her head, "well, two different *beings*, but her magic is yours. You're in the driver's seat." She crosses her arms, lifting an eyebrow. "At least for now."

My body freezes. Does she know? No, she couldn't. This is my internal struggle, and I have yet to voice what is actually happening. I allow my body to relax, mirror her movements, and cross my own arms. "For now?"

Her eyes narrow, pausing in her response. "Yes."

Sighing, I drop my arms back to my sides and turn back to the portal. Eventually, I'll tell her how right she is, but not yet. I would like to figure out what the heck is going on myself, before I start voicing my concerns and knowledge to other people. Besides, it's a burden I'm supposed to be enduring myself, not bringing others into.

"Where do you think this leads?" I whisper.

She doesn't answer right away, but I hear her shuffle her feet. "Anywhere you wish. Even realms."

I take a step forward, but I'm halted from going beyond that, and not by my own body and mind. Myla stopped my movements. I try to mask my fright, knowing this will sound alarm bells and drive home Tember's previously voiced thoughts.

Myla does have control over me, more than Tember realizes and possibly more than I even realize. She's probably frightened I'll go to Corbin. Without him being in my presence, I don't feel that pull. Mild curiosity is what drove me forward, but I doubt she'll allow that chance again.

Taking a step back, I adjust my shirt, busying my shaking fingers. "Best not to explore just yet."

Lifting my arm, or rather, Myla lifts my arm; my hand stretches upward, parallel with the vortex portal. In a slow small circle, she waves my hand, and the portal fizzles out with a pop.

CHAPTER EIGHT

KATRIANE DUPONT

EARTH REALM

The beeping from the grocery store registers ring against my ears, a headache forming underneath my entire scalp. Each time they scan an item, it's a fight not to cringe as I examine the fruit.

Grocery stores calm me. The smell, the normality—it eases my anxiety.

I used to work in a grocery store to earn extra cash. My coven never allowed me to buy the style of clothes of my choice, so in order to wear what I wanted, I had to buy them on my own.

Working as a clerk was my first job, and it was one I enjoyed. Being around normal people, feeling like I wasn't so different than the average person, gave me a sense of belonging, which is something that comes in short supply these days.

Everywhere I look, there's a new discovery, a new unwanted adventure. I'd give anything to be normal right now, even if that meant working as a grocery store cashier for the rest of my life.

Placing some plums into a bag, I look over at Tember. She's holding an orange under the light, twisting it within her fingers with the look of concentration squinting her eyes.

"What are you doing?" I ask, a smile forming.

"How do you get the food out of this ball?" she whispers.

A plump, gray-haired woman passing behind her sucks her lips between her teeth, desperately trying not to laugh as she pushes her cart down the aisle.

"It's called an orange." I take the fruit from her, snap a plastic bag from its holder, and place it inside. "You peel it first."

Tember frowns, watching as I set it inside the cart. "Food named after a color . . ." She glances at the rest of the fruit, grabbing a peach in a swift motion. "Is this an orange as well?"

My tongue flicks out before scraping my top lip with my teeth. Closing my eyes briefly, I turn from her, choosing to ignore the question and pushing the cart to the rows of neatly stacked vegetables.

She continues, "Are all your foods named after colors or are the colors named after your foods?" She stops as soon she sees rows of shelves containing green vegetables. "I void my last question." She picks up a stock of broccoli before frowning and taking a sniff. "You eat trees?"

My head goes limp, and I laugh under my breath. Snatching the broccoli from her grasps, I set it in the cart before grabbing a few more items. "I will teach you our ways." She opens her mouth to say something else, but I cut her off with a finger. "At home." I look at her pointedly.

****

The scent of rain is in the air, but thankfully, it is still holding off. Tember carries most of the groceries, her request, while we walk side by side down the sidewalk.

Tall, old buildings reach toward the night sky, and if you watch them too long, they look to be swaying in the breeze. Maybe they are. Maybe nothing is stable in this realm, perhaps in all the realms.

A chilly breeze runs up my back, and I pull my coat tighter around me. The plastic bags full of food crackle with the extra movement, bouncing against my sides.

I look at Tember, frowning at her apparel. "Aren't you cold?"

"Angels don't feel—" she begins.

I roll my eyes. "Pain." So she keeps reminding me. What I would give to not feel pain. "Do you feel, like . . . pleasure?"

She nods under poncho hood. "Yes."

The words pop out of my mouth before my mind can filter them. "So, angels have sex then?"

She laughs. My cheeks flush a bright pink, and I look away. "Yes. We enjoy pleasurable experiences just as much as humans do."

I don't bother nodding. Having already embarrassed myself to the point of being tongue-tied, I figure it's best to keep my mouth shut at this point.

Our feet echo against the pavement as we walk in tune with each other. It's late and the city is sleeping, so when her voice pops into my head, my steps falter.

You're being followed.

I slow my pace while trying to use my peripheral vision to view the potential threat. I don't see anything which causes slight fear to puddle in my stomach. Eyeing an alley just ahead, I fumble with my grocery bags between my fingers.

"What's wrong?" Tember asks, noticing my nervous fidgeting.

Another bout of rain begins as I turn into the alley, ducking under the bright yellow caution tape. Down the street, I hear the downpour as it pounds against each surface it comes in contact with.

Judging by the yellow caution tape, it looks like there was a crime scene here at one point. How ironic that there may be another.

"In here," I whisper, switching the bags to one hand and holding up the tape. Tember ducks and steps into the alley with me, doubt thinning her lips.

"What's going on, Kat?" she whispers, glancing down the alley.

"We're being followed." I peek around the side of the brick building.

"How do you know?"

I glance back at her, flattening my back against the wall while glaring. Always so much doubt. My coat snags on a few sharp pieces of brick, but I ignore it. "She told me."

Tember searches my eyes, her jaw clenching. "She speaks to you?"

I'm cut off mid-nod when several figures drop from the roof down the way. Their red eyes tell me enough—vampires.

Not wasting a moment, my face begins to distort, and my eyes glow an orange hue, slightly illuminating the open space in front of me.

Tember cocks her head while looking at me before her face relaxes, and she slowly swivels to the figures behind her. She shifts her body to face them before gently setting the bags on the ground. I follow her lead, placing my groceries next to hers.

"What's the plan?" she asks.

I open my mouth to answer, but another voice replaces it, coming from within. "There is no plan," Myla says.

I'm gently eased back inside my mind while she takes over my body, my movements, my speech. It's unsettling, frightening. Yet, that damn curiosity I have cocks its head, waiting to see what happens next. I was fully prepared to do what I could to erase this threat, but at the same time, I want to know if the beast is controllable. It has to be, right? So far, Myla's spirit—Myla's dragon—has done nothing to harm me. Maybe this is her way of keeping me safe?

Tember tenses at my voice's change in pitch but doesn't turn around. "Hello, Myla," she says with casual ease.

It's like I'm watching a movie. I have no control over my actions. Unlike the time in the woods, I'm still in my body. The rate of this progression and her demanding control over my body is terrifying. More so than the stalking, walking dead.

My hand is lifted, a ball of flames circling in my palm. Myla watches it, and I feel a grin spread across my face.

What are you doing? I ask her, a nervous tick in my tone.

135

Myla answers aloud, "Kheelan knows. They're here for me. For you. I won't let them take us."

Tember shifts slightly, her ear more centered, listening to what Myla said. "Myla, you need to give her body back," she mumbles.

Hovering my other hand above the ball of flame, Myla doesn't answer. Instead, she lifts my top hand, and as she does so, the ball changes from baseball to basketball size. Tendrils of flame continue to swirl in a sphere, a few try to escape, licking the air before they fizzle out. It crackles like sparklers, and the larger it grows, the louder it gets.

Myla blows on the ball with a gentle breeze. The ball flies from my hand, much faster than it should, and hits the first advancing vampire. He combusts into flames, his screams echoing off the brick wall before a pile of ash is all that's left.

Resolved to the fact that Myla won't allow me the control, Tember runs forward and skids to her knees, meeting the rest head on. She holds out her hand, and a black bow appears in her grasp. It's extremely large in size and looks to be just as heavy, but she holds it with ease.

Tember aims the bow and an arrow, crackling with electricity, appears just before she releases the string. The arrow sails, whistling while it cuts through the wind and rain, before turning more into a lightning bolt than wooden arrow. It buries itself in the chest of the vampire with a thud, lighting him up like a firework.

I wait impatiently inside my body, hoping Myla does something soon. If I were to guess, I'd say she never saw an angel in action. Well, that makes two of us. It's fascinating to watch, but unfortunately, we don't have the luxury to.

The vampires continue to close in on us, the majority more interested in me than the arrow-welding angel on the ground picking them off one by one. There's no way one witch can take on this many vampires, even the First Born.

A smile spreads across my cheeks, pulling the distorted skin around my eyes. "Don't be afraid," Myla mumbles. I'm not sure if she's talking to me or if she's talking to herself. The silent debate I have over her statement quickly disappears as I feel Myla begin to change my body.

I grow, at least twenty feet taller, and as I do, my bones crack in the most excruciating way. Everything grows smaller, or so it seems. My skin itches like I'm being bitten by a thousand tiny ants, and internally, I scream. I feel the same sensations I did that day in the woods—the heat, the blossoming of pain inside my skull . . . everything.

As the pain begins to subside, large muscles ripple and quiver around every bone. I'm standing on all fours, puffs of smoke leaving my long muzzle. My tail swings, hitting the wall and a few crumbles of brick fall to the ground.

A little knocked off kilter, I swing my long neck to the side, viewing my tail before shifting it back to the threat. I'm in control over my body, over the dragon. Myla has retreated inside, a smug reaction coming from her emotions. Did she do this to prove a point?

I double blink, disoriented. My vision is sharper, I can see every black vein, in frightening detail, crawling across the vampires' skin.

They've paused their advance, and for the first time in my life, due to me, I see fear on the vampires' face. Adrenaline pumps through this dragon form, and I marvel at it. I feel invincible, indestructible. It should be a terrifying feeling, but I can't help but delightfully bask in it.

I shake my head and snort, feeling the fins of spikes wave against my spine and each muscle's power underneath my scales. It brings me back to the memory and my earlier fear of Myla's dragon. I will fear this creature no more. This is who I am. This is what I am. This dragon is *mine.*

Myla laughs inside my head, enjoying the show and my thoughts.

Tember still plucks away at them, but I can see her eyes constantly shifting back and forth between my dragon form and the threat. They've forgotten about her, no longer seeing her as the target, which makes it easier for her to pick them off. But I don't plan to let her take all the glory.

I step my front claw forward, the nails scraping against the concrete, and draw in a large breath. My ribs expand, and heat builds inside my chest. The feeling is glorious, unlike any other—it's power and comfort all in one, yet almost too hot, too scorching, before I'm forced to blow it out. As it leaves my throat, passes my rows of sharp teeth, plumes of smoke go with it, temporarily clouding my vision. The flames leave my muzzle like a torch, and it almost sounds like one, too.

The fire hits the first vampire, engulfing him, before I lower my head and shift it from side to side. One by one, the vampires ignite, each taking turns littering the cement with piles of ash. My adrenaline kicks up a notch, victory now fueling it.

I take in the scene, anxious for more, as a crack of thunder vibrates against my scales. The street is lit by the remaining vampires who still hold on, screeching inhuman wails and flailing their arms engulfed in flames. The last one dusts and my roar of victory matches that of the storm.

As the last of my roar comes to an end, I snort and stomp my foot. Tiny pebbles quiver against the ground, and the piles of ash flatten themselves against the force of my weight. My head swings over to Tember, who still aims her bow. She looks frozen, terrified, but her eyes hold wonder as she looks back at me.

She lowers the bow and hesitates for a moment before taking a step forward. "Kat?" she whispers.

I drop my head closer to the ground as she takes baby steps in my direction. Two feet from me, she glances at her bow before it disappears from her hand the same way it had appeared. Using the same hand, she reaches forward, her fingers twitching in the air.

A snort leaves my throat, fanning her hair as it travels through my nostrils. For goodness sake, I'm not a rabid beast. I mentally giggle at that. Wasn't I just the one who was thinking the opposite?

I shove my muzzle into her outstretched hand, proving my point and causing her to jump slightly. After a moment, she smiles and runs it against my black scales. It's at this moment that I understand why cats like to have their heads scratched. As her fingers trail over the scales, it's the most delicious relief to the itch I never knew I had.

Sirens wail in the distance and our heads snap to attention, my fins of spikes flattening against my scales.

"Do you know how to change back?" Tember asks, desperation in her voice.

Most likely, someone heard the racket we were making. I don't know how they'll explain the piles of ash, but the downpour should continue to carry them away.

I think for a moment until I realize I don't know how to change back. Myla has always been the one to initiate it.

All you must do is ask, my daughter, she replies. Her voice is so loving it throws me. Is it possible since now I've accepted her being here, she's accepted me in return?

Her magic pulses through me like a second heartbeat before the bones begin to shrivel, crack, reshape, until finally, I'm settled on my own two feet . . . naked.

The transformation will hurt less and less over time, she whispers.

She's right. This time it was only a dull ache as I returned to human form. However, all the adrenaline my dragon half had dissipated with it. My earlier anxiety returns, my bravado gone. What I'd give to keep a little of that extra 'fire' inside me at all times. Maybe then I wouldn't hesitate with actions in the future.

The sirens grow closer as I cover my bits, my fingers fumbling to hide the modest portions of myself.

"Do you have any extra clothes?" Tember asks, her tone edgy.

Anxiety comes through my voice, controlling my words as I snap, "Do I look like I brought an extra set of clothes? Does it look like I had plans of turning into a fire-breathing dragon?" I bounce on my toes, trying to warm myself. "Shit! What do we do now?"

Tember's eyes narrow as she stares at me. The words seem forced like she doesn't want to say them. "The portal."

"I need some form of evaporation," I growl, my teeth beginning to chatter.

She glances around before her eyes relax with glee. I follow her line of vision to the street where a drain is built into the curb. Steam roles out of it before disappearing into the cold rain.

I shake my head in quick motions. "No. No, absolutely not. I'm naked! I can't just walk into the street like this." I stomp my foot like a child. "What if someone sees?"

She lifts an eyebrow. "Would you rather tell the authorities what you're doing in an alley, naked, with several bags of groceries and piles of vampire ash?"

My eyebrows dip, and a sneer crosses my lips. Mumbling under my breath, I step over to the edge of the wall and peek both ways. Seeing no living person, cars, or walkers, I duck under the tape and tiptoe to the street drain. I hesitate for a moment before uncovering my breasts, mumbling curses under my breath.

Holding my hands over the drain, I capture the steam, just as I did in the shop, and form flames with it by blowing inside my cupped hands. I let the ball hover in my palms, carefully cradling it like a flighty butterfly, before I tiptoe back to Tember with haste.

A pebble already between her fingers, she glances at me before dropping it inside the ball. I blow, and it transforms just like before. As the portal grows into a swirling circle of red and orange, misting flames, she grabs the drenched groceries from the ground.

"Ready?" she asks. Her posture is confident, mine less so. I've never done this before.

My voice cracks after I swallow my fear. "How?"

She looks at the portal and steps forward. "Think of the place you want to go, and step through."

I step forward to meet her and grab the edge of her elbow. The sirens echo just down the road. We take hurried steps, passing inside the portal while I picture my apartment living room.

CHAPTER NINE

AIDEN VANDER

THE TWEEN

"Where am I?" I ask. I've never been here before. A place like this doesn't exist.

Jane tilts her head, her eyes flicking to the side of my face. "The Tween."

The side of my lips tilts up in mockery. "The Tween?"

"Yes." She hesitates. "It's the voided area between the Earth Realm." She pauses, turning her head and mumbling her next words, "And the Death Realm."

My head whips to hers. "No Heaven or Hell?"

She shakes her head, her hair waving and fanning the area with the scent of roses. "No, dear."

I glance around, my jaw flexing once at such a drastic change to my previous existence. I've never been good with changes. Maybe that's why I stuck with the same routine as a human even though I loathed it.

The Tween looks just like Earth, except swirls of fog and mist float about, licking the moss-covered, gnarled tree trunks of the forest we stand in. There are no earthy smells here, no sounds of life. Birds should be singing, flapping their wings as they bounce from tree to tree. Squirrels should be collecting nuts at the base of every trunk before cursing us in their native tongue. Bugs should be buzzing about their busy tasks.

But they're not. They don't exist here. This isn't a place for beating hearts.

Jane takes a deep breath and gives a shake of her head, forcing a smile. She takes a step forward. "Ready?" My mind flashes back to those same words she said in the alley. I can almost hear the sirens again.

I nod, unsure but willing. Where else am I going to go? I clear my throat unnecessarily. "How was I able to dream about you . . . about where I would . . ." I flex my jaw, "die?"

Fallen branches pass through our skin—it's pointless to avoid them by lifting our feet. She tilts her head, considering her next words carefully, as she continues walking in front of me. "I'm a shade—you're a shade. The Earth Realm and the Death Realm are mixing, making it possible to cross over."

I frown. "Mixing? How?"

"No one knows," she mumbles, etched with warm concern. "It's never happened before."

I'm just about to question her again when she stops, searching the open space available between the trees, her head swiveling this way and that.

"What are we waiting for?" I ask, my voice rumbling as I glance around and see nothing but a lifeless forest.

She doesn't answer. As we wait, I shift my weightless body uncomfortably. Her head snaps to the side, and I follow her line of vision.

Two figures off in the distance walk with unhurried steps. A slow smile spreads across Jane's face as they get closer.

A brown-haired man, lanky but muscular, is ahead of another. A wide, goofy, lopsided smile shows straight, pearly-white teeth. His hair is cropped short and he's transparent—a shade, just like me. Bruises around his neck and wrists are visible, providing me with evidence of his death. What a death that must have been, to die with a noose around your neck.

I glance at my sweatshirt. The blood is gone, the hole the knife made no longer visible to the naked eye. I touch the surface of the cloth, feeling jagged skin underneath where the knife had entered my heart, ending my life.

I look behind him. A woman shuffles along, her steps tentative, unsure, and her eyes are on mine as she pulls at her invisible fingers. She's older—about the age of Jane. No evidence of her death can be seen.

With any luck, this woman died in her sleep. That was the way I wanted to leave that world. No one should be put through the knowledge that a single breath could be their last.

"Dyson," Jane says, the name a warm embrace by itself, like the first time she said mine.

"Jane." He nods, his smile still on his face.

She pulls him into a hug before pulling back, her hands gripping his shoulders. "Tanya," Jane greets the woman who stopped just short behind Dyson.

Dyson blinks with happy eyes as he watches Jane peck Tanya's cheek. I glance at the woman, my eyebrows scrunching together.

"Aiden," Jane begins, and I shift my eyes to her. "This is your mother—your real mother—Tanya."

I blink at Jane. My eyelids flutter rapidly as her words sink in before I slowly shift my head back to the woman who gave birth to me.

Her eyes are lowered, staring at her fingers as they pull one another, before she raises them to mine. They're dewy, wet with tears about to spill over the rims. She hesitates before taking a step forward.

Emotions travel through my invisible body—emotions I haven't felt in years. I've been blocking those feelings since before I can remember. They lick my insides—or whatever it is now that I'm a shade—and tempt me to feel more, constricting my throat and pricking my eyes. I buck against it for a moment before I shove my mental block aside.

Tanya takes another step and pulls her fingers apart, lifts her hand, and cups my cheek. "My boy," she whispers, longing in her voice.

My eyes search hers, my body rigid before a tear spills over, traveling down to the square of my jaw. "Mom?"

I've never met her, and my foster family, the Tillers, knew nothing about her. There was no information to be found—why she didn't want me, why I never knew who she was, why she left me in the care of strangers as a baby. I often dreamed of this day, but this wasn't how I pictured our first meeting. Death wasn't what I had envisioned I needed to gain a family.

She smiles, and the rims of her lids no longer hold her tears. Wiping at them with her thumb, she inclines her head. "Yes."

My eyelids close, and I lean into her palm, placing my hand over hers. She drops her hand and wraps her arms around my waist. Sobs wrack her body, and her frame shakes against my chest. I return the embrace before opening my eyes, staring at Jane and Dyson. They're smiling, delighted with the reunion.

Tanya, my mother, pulls away from me after several minutes and pecks my cheek. I have so many questions for her, so many things I need to be answered. But that can wait. I have an eternity to ask them. This is death, and death is endless.

She folds her hand in mine before turning a watery smile toward Dyson and Jane. "Thank you," she says to them. Jane nods her head, her hand flying to her trembling bottom lip as Dyson's lopsided, goofy grin reappears.

"So . . . what now?" I cough, clearing the lump from my throat.

"Now we begin our plan." Dyson's face relaxes as his eyes search mine. "Something is happening on the Earth Realm. Something that's shifting our worlds together." His eyes glow a shade of green. "I'd take a wild guess and say that we aren't the only realms that have merged."

Startled, my head shakes a little. "Your eyes are glowing."

He scratches his cheek and the green glow fades. "I was a . . . I was a wolf-shifter. Before . . ."

I double blink, feeling out of place, out of touch, uninformed . . . like I've been thrown into an alternate reality. I suppose I have. I find myself having a hard time keeping up with what I'm being shown, what I'm being told, and this other world I never knew existed.

Wolf-shifters are real? I suppose it's not far-fetched. "Wolf-shifters, ghosts . . . what else is there?" I glance at Jane while my mother rubs my arm soothingly, aware of my distress.

Her lips form a hard line. "We prefer to be called shades, dear. And there are a great deal of legends that exist across the realms."

Dyson continues as if I never asked the question, "Things are about to change around here. We need all the help we can get."

My eyebrows scrunch together once more, and I glance over at him. "Change? How?"

Frowning, he shifts his weight, glancing at the forest floor. "It's complicated. But before we get into the details . . ." He looks at Jane. The tilt of his head displays more detail of the bruising along his neck.

What happened to this guy? Obviously, he was hung, but why? Who would do such a thing to a person?

Jane lowers her hand from her mouth, clearing her throat. "I need a favor from you."

"A favor?" I just got here. What kind of favor can you ask a gho—a shade?

My mother turns to me. "Jane's daughter . . . She's about to go through the same fate as you—"

"Death?" I ask, quirking a brow and finishing her sentence.

She nods. "Yes. Jane . . . she can't—"

"I can't be the one to get her," Jane interrupts. "Eliza, my daughter, she's angry with me. I left her alone when I . . ."

My face relaxes as realization clicks. "You think she'll fight the dream if she sees you."

Jane nods, her bottom lip trembling. I think, biting the inside of my lip. "Okay. I'll do this," I agree and incline my head toward Jane, "for you."

Her eyes close in relief, and my mother grips my hand tighter.

I mentally prepare myself, stretching my neck. "How do I do it?"

Dyson steps forward. "I can help with that." He lifts his hand before stopping, suspending it in mid-air. "This may be disorienting. The jump between two –realms—the space between it . . . it's not meant to be traveled."

"The dreams?" I ask, remembering how real it was.

Dyson nods, the movement exaggerated. I get the feeling that's a character trait. He seems the type to not hurt a fly. "You may forget your reasoning, but you won't be able to return here if she leaves the dream."

A little nervous about what I've agreed to, I gulp, flex my jaw, and nod.

"We'll wait for you here," my mother whispers.

He bends, twirling his finger in the cold fog at the base of the forest floor. The fog responds, slithering over his skin like a pet snake greeting its owner. My eyes grow wide as I tilt my head, blinking several times to make sure I'm seeing what I'm actually seeing.

Dyson stands, holding out his palm, face up. The fog gives one more caress to his forearm and then travels through the air, landing on my shoulder before growing. It swirls around me, through me, and I feel the pull—the same pull from my dream—tugging at my torso. My mother squeezes my hand once more before I'm gone.

TEMBER

EARTH REALM

The sandman fidgets, pulling his unusually long fingers. "Sureen grows suspicious."

I scoff. Sureen is the Fee of the Dream Realm. She's strict, often running her realm as though the sandmen are mere tools. Continuously screening her sandmen for any surfacing emotions as well as details they obtain while on the Earth Realm, she's known for her iron fist and quick backlash.

Around the time Myla was hung as a witch, Erline and Sureen had a disagreement. It concluded with an eternal grudge. Sureen, the paranoid fool, created creatures and used them as Earth watchdogs. She forces them to remain without emotion so they have no quarrels about relaying any information. I'd wager they don't even know they're being forced to do anything.

A few hundred years ago, Sureen sent a sandman to the village Myla lived in. She instructed the sandman to manipulate his dreamer's dreams, forcing him to see Myla as a witch and spread suspicion like a plague. I wasn't there, but I heard the rumors just the same. The dreamer watched through the window of Myla's home, catching her in the act as she used her magic, and she was sentenced to death for witchcraft.

The man's name was Gandalf. I remember because when Erma retells the story, she feels pity for the poor man. Kheelan took Gandalf for himself, desperate for answers and eternal punishment within his realm.

Erline always had a kind soul, but since she lost her only daughter, she's been put away, occasionally wreaking havoc on her creations with powerful storms. She's put Sureen away in a tiny metaphorical box, never mentioning her, never letting that name cross her lips, but at the same time, she blames the humans. Those were the hands that ended her daughter's life.

I suppose one could say Erline and Sureen both hold a grudge. Fee aren't known for their humanity or humility. They take what they want when they want it. I know better than to believe Erma, my Fee creator, isn't this way, but I love her anyway. We can't choose who our heart's want. Angels are known for wearing their hearts on their sleeves . . . in more ways than one.

The sandman continues to pull his fingers while my eyes remain glued to the nervous movement. "Tell me, are you feeling anything?" My eyes snap to his. "Anything you shouldn't?"

He pauses in his finger pulling, settling his hands back to his sides as if those very words reminded him of who he's supposed to be. Reluctantly, he answers, "Yes."

I tilt my head to the side. "Interesting. And you've always been Kat's sandman?"

"Yes," he answers with more confidence, straightening his spine.

I shake my head, getting back to the previous topic. "A few more times. A few more times, and I won't ask this favor of you again. It's important that she has all the information she needs."

He shifts his head to the side, his eyes narrowing around their white depths. "Information she needs or information *you* need? Are you here to spy, angel?"

I glare at him, my eyes holding the steel of a challenge. The clock along the wall ticks for several Earth seconds. Nodding, he turns on his large heel and leaves the living room, heading down the hall.

My mind flits through what he said. He's having feelings—emotions—when he shouldn't. It is probable that this is what Sureen is suspicious about. The vampires clearly know she's alive—why else would she be hunted. Kheelan knows Myla's alive, and he sent them here to find her. It stands to reason that Sureen would grow curious, pushing her sandmen for further answers. Surely her sandmen have told her about the uprising in vampires, but I wonder how much Kat's sandman told her.

The sandman's accusation pops back into my thoughts. I quietly scoff, refusing to believe I'm here for only myself. My intentions aren't selfish.

I sniff, rubbing my nose and going over the events that I've partaken in since I arrive. The sandman planted a seed of doubt within me.

Watching as he sprinkles his dream dust on her face and her nose twitches, my mind flits through most of my life and the charges I've watched over. I've never lost one, never. The only time they've left my care through death was by natural causes.

He turns to me and begins to nod when the world slows almost to a halt.

My movements become minute, and a slow look of shock crosses the sandman's face. For a moment, I'm confused. What's happening?

A shimmering wave develops behind the sandman. He starts to turn his head, noticing his backside is no longer unoccupied. A woman stands there, as dark as night just like the sandman, except her eyes are the same color as her skin. She's tall with long shapely legs and hair pinned back in tight braids along her scalp. Her movements are much faster than mine and the sluggish world she's manipulated.

Her top lip curls against her smooth skin, and she sneers at me before turning her dark eyes on a sleeping Kat. Her lips move in rapid pace, but I'm unable to hear the words spilling from her mouth. I take a step forward, but it's of no use. By the time my first step reaches the ground, she's gone and the sandman with her.

Sureen. Sureen figured it out.

CHAPTER TEN

KATRIANE DUPONT

MYLA'S MEMORIES

The citizens pull her through the doorway of iron bars, shouting and screaming curses in French. Fists are raised, waving with vigor in the air, and a gentle breeze blows the flames of the torches lit amongst the crowd.

Instead of being inside the cage with Myla, I'm among the ever-moving crowd. Spittle hits the back of my neck, but that's not what scares me out of my wits, raising my heart rate and sending fear to my toes.

What scares me is, as the crowd pushes like an angry mob, I'm being jostled to and fro. I'm no longer an innocent bystander, unseen by the naked eye. I'm in the crowd. I'm part of the crowd.

Dread rocks my core, bubbling inside me and threatening to spill from my mouth with a blood-curdling scream. My head swivels from side to side, taking in each face full of malice before flitting to the next. I gulp before turning my attention to the very thing they're cursing at.

Two men continue to haul Myla toward the steps of the gallows, one of them I recognize as the peeper from Myla's window. His long hair is unkempt, a rat's nest formed at the back of his head. She doesn't fight them but instead keeps her back straight with pride. She saved these people, and she knows it. Her steps up each board are drowned out by the screams and anger. No one speaks against it. No one shouts that killing a person is wrong, protesting to spare a life. No one steps forward to save their savior.

Stopping next to the hanging noose, they turn her and our eyes lock. I suck in a breath because the woman who's staring at me isn't 'past' Myla. The beautiful blond witch who holds my gaze is 'present' Myla . . . well, my present. I don't know how I know. I just do. When you spend the last few months sharing a mind with another being, you tend to know her on more than a friendly personal level.

Recognition is written all over her features, and she's not surprised to see me. A sad smile crosses her lips, and I take a step forward. She whispers the word, "no," but I can't hear it. The shouting around me consumes the vibrations of my eardrums. I hesitate, my lips closing as I swallow a barrelful of guilt. Should I save her? Can I save her?

My mind works quickly, my eyes scanning her face. If I'm visible here, if I'm rooted to this spot and so is she, won't that change history? If I try to stop it?

Tears well in my eyes, blurring my vision. I may not have acknowledged her existence with grace, but she's still family. No, she's right. She must carry on with this. If she doesn't, my entire history would change. I could not exist. The world could not exist. If she doesn't play this out the same way she did in the past, everything could be lost. She's not willing to take that chance, and regretfully, I agree.

A tear spills over my cheek, trickling down the skin with an icy chill, and I take a deep breath, desperate to ease the lump that blocks its way. My chest hurts like my heart is breaking and scattering into tiny pieces. Myla's eyes briefly close, a sign of relief that I understand without her having to voice it.

Her focus stays on me as they hook the noose over her neck.

The crowd dies down, murmuring their words and curses while a man speaks next to Myla, "We're lucky that Gandalf discovered the devil's child. Any last words, beast?"

If crickets were still alive, I imagine they'd be the only things chirping in the background right now, the crowd is so silent. They wait for her to speak, wait to hang on to every last word she says so they can later mock them while they drink with victory.

People can be filled with such evil, no matter their make. True sincerity is rare to find amongst those who were made for it.

"My daughter's daughter will be my legacy." Her voice is gentle but thick with emotion. "She'll have all my gifts, without the burden of me. She will be what saves this realm from those who threaten its existence."

The crowd holds its breath as the people work through the meaning of her words. They were spoken in English, and I have my doubts that anyone here actually speaks it. The only sound is their torches flickering in the night. Double blinking, my mind halts for just a moment. Daughter—as in singular . . . but she has twins. Is she talking about them? Or . . . or is she talking to me?

Shaking his head, a nervous laugh erupts from the man's throat. "You're a crazy witch, aren't you?"

Someone behind me shouts, "The tongue of the Devil himself!"

Gandalf, the one who caught her magic, pushes her back so she's just under the wooden bar that the thick, roped noose is wrapped around. My stomach flip-flops, threatening to upchuck everything I ate, and my heart thumps at rapid speed. Every bone in my body wants to move forward, to save her from this madness, but my brain refuses the action.

The knot forming in my throat loosens, and a sob escapes me.

A tiny tear glistens against her cheek, reflecting the flickering flames of the torches surrounding Myla. She closes her eyes as the man nods at a Gandalf, who's holding a lever behind her.

I step forward, hand outstretched, but my muscles freeze, halted as he yanks the lever back. My heart shatters, no longer whole.

A loud crack in the wood screeches violently against my ears before the trapdoor is dropped. Myla falls, dropping with it, the rope tightening around her neck. With her hands tied behind her, her feet kick with desperation, searching for purchase of any kind.

The rational side of my brain recognizes it as the fight or flight response. It's nature, the fight to live. Even until your last breath.

Her face turns a violent shade of lavender, her lips a dark blue. She blinks, and I see the veins bursting in the whites of her eyes. Beautiful blond hair swings back and forth with gentle ease, even as her body fights for one last breath of vital oxygen.

****

They take her from the noose, unwrapping it with an ease they didn't have before. I'm rooted to my spot, frozen in a state of terror. They killed her. She's dead. Hung for being a witch.

The last thought crosses my mind, echoing, stirring me from my paralyzed state. I begin backing away from the scene, knowing I can't stay here, especially dressed like this. Someone will notice, someone will think it odd, and someone will surely delve deeper into who I am and how I got here.

With no better idea of where to go, I turn and head toward Myla's home. My slow walk turns into a desperate jog, the hard-packed dirt pattering against my hard-soled boots. The door protests as I turn the knob and slip inside.

The house is warm, safe. It's Myla's home. This is the place she slept, gave birth to her girls, and created a family. This is where my heritage began. And it was ripped from her by a single rope and an angry mob that couldn't accept they were saved by someone different than them.

I lean my back against the doorframe, my breaths coming heavy. My head thumps against the wood as I thrust it back, holding back a scream of anger.

A tickle on my cheek causes my hand to raise and scrape at it. I pull it away when I feel wetness and hold it in front of my face. My fingers are soaked in my own tears. I bet I was the only one to cry for her.

How could they be so cruel? Myla had saved them from the largest horde of vampires I've ever seen. Without her, they'd all be dead, and this town would be forgotten. She saved them, yet they're too blind to see it.

I sniffle and glance around, wiping my nose with the heel of my palm. The girls are gone. No doubt Erline has already come to collect them, stuffing them away and burying the secrets. The angry side of me begins to blame her for not saving her only daughter. If she loved her so much, why couldn't she do more? I understand the fate of the witches was what started this whole mess. Or perhaps, she allowed her daughter to die because Myla wished it. Puzzle pieces aren't fitting together, and it's beginning to piss me off that I'm left in the dark.

A glint above the fireplace catches my eye. Since the room is so dark, I automatically fumble for a light switch before I realize what time period I'm in.

Hysterical giggles leave my throat followed by a scoff of ignorance. It sounds foreign, something that would never come from my own mouth. Perhaps I'm in shock.

I quickly search for a candle, which isn't hard to find. My fingers fumble aimlessly on the short table next to the door before they touch the cold brass of the candle holder.

Glancing at the windows, I look for peekers before lighting a small flame in my hand. To my surprise, the ball ignites. A small part of me thought Myla's powers, and the dragon, would have died along with her. Maybe she was talking to me after all.

I don't feel the dragon in me, not like I did when I shared my body. Could it be that we've mended, molded, into one being? Time will tell. For a split moment, I fear the dragon may be gone, but the flaming ball in my hand tells me to think rationally. I wouldn't be able to conjure it without a spell if I were but a simple witch now. A small tendril of relief eases my aching heart that I still have a small piece of her left behind for me to call my own.

The ball hovers before I settle it on the wick. Picking up the candle holder, I swing back around and step over to the fireplace, determined to find what caught my interest, anything for a distraction.

Above the mantle, a piece of metal décor adorns the shiplap wall. I lift the candle higher to get the full view.

It's a half moon, exactly like my ex-coven's crescent. However, there is one difference. There's no strike through it. Perhaps . . . perhaps, the strike is symbolic.

From what I remember in our lessons, Myla was the first witch to be executed. A long line of daughters followed. Could the strike stand for that? A strike against inhumanity? It's probable. No one actually knows what the strike means, but none of them witnessed what happened, either. How did her legacy carry on with no one left to voice it?

My eyes close as understanding hits me like a boulder. Bending to the fireplace, I rub my fingertips in the soot before standing once more. I hesitate before lifting black soiled fingers to the metal half-moon. In a slow swipe, I create the strike meant for the crescent.

Time travel works in mysterious ways. Is it a coincidence I was brought here? No. Coincidences are for those who don't want to believe that everything is connected. They fear the truth and create the excuse. The truth is simple: one fate is connected to another's. To some, that's scarier than death itself.

"Who are you?" a male tenor rumbles behind me.

I scream, the unexpected intrusion skipping beats within the chambers of my aching heart. My body jumps and spins in mid-air, a flaming ball at the ready before it soars from my hand, straight at the unexpected visitor.

The man ducks, and the flickering ball flies into the wall, igniting it with flames. He stands from his crouched position and waves an arm, causing the flames to disappear before my eyes. I glance from the fully repaired wall to the man, my fried brain acknowledging that this isn't a human who stands before me.

Corbin straightens his back before crossing his arms over his chest, a feral glare contorting his face with unvoiced reprimand.

He eyes the next flaming ball in my hands, watches it lick my palms, crackle and sizzle, before his eyes lift back to mine. He's just as handsome as I remember from Myla's memories and seeing him across the street from my shop. To be here in person, to be standing this close, I'd be lying if I said goosebumps didn't raise over my skin.

I close my palm, the fire extinguishing within it.

"Kat." I clear my throat. "My name is Kat."

He snarls like a rabid dog, his white teeth shining in the candlelight. "What are you doing in my home, Kat?"

CHAPTER ELEVEN

TEMBER

EARTH REALM

I pace the living room, certain I'm wearing the wood floors thin. Checking the clock again, I turn and walk the length once more. It's past the normal time Kat wakes. Her alarm has chirped and silenced three times. The store is due to be open at any moment, and Kat has yet to wake.

Growling under my breath, I uncurl my arms from around my torso and stomp down the short hall to Kat's room. The door is left open from last night's visit, so I don't bother with Earth's modesty of knocking before entering.

I stand inside her doorway. "Kat." She's in the exact same position as she was last night. "Kat," I say a little louder.

She doesn't move, doesn't twitch or budge. Her eyelids don't even flutter. I cross the short distance to her and grab her shoulder, saying her name once more.

As I'm shaking her, panic begins to curl my insides. My hand moves from her shoulder to the pulse in her neck, my fingers trembling until they feel a steady beat. I blow out a pent-up breath I didn't notice I was holding.

"Kat!" I scream. I curse in every language I know. Did something go wrong when Sureen took away the sandman? The words she mumbled before she disappeared . . . Did she do something to Kat?

I pace the bedroom this time, keeping a constant eye on Kat while forming a frantic plan. My mind is jumbled—nothing makes sense except that I'm the root cause of this.

The sandman was right—this was a selfish act. How can I call myself an Angel when my acts aren't pure?

The only thought in my head that makes any sense is: How do I wake someone under a Fee spell?

AIDEN VANDER

THE TWEEN

Thick, unnatural fog, so heavy I can't see through it, threatens to consume me. If I were still breathing for the sole purpose of oxygen, I imagine it'd be nearly impossible. It bellows and sways, obscuring the view of what's behind it. There are no smells here, nothing to grasp for evidence.

Where am I? How did I get here? I stuff my hands into my pockets. I lower my head, seeing nothing but the cold, twirling fog, trying to remember. My eyebrows knit together in concentration.

I hear the breeze play with trees, the sound unmistakable. Am I in a forest?

"Hel—?" I hear a voice call, the tone so frightened, so eager for answers. I frown, wondering if my mind is playing tricks on me—if this is all but a dream.

A twig breaks, and I blink. "Hello?" the voice calls again—a caressing, quiet voice.

Slowly, I lift my head. The fog has parted, creating a path to the woman walking toward me from the other end. My eyes lock on hers, and she stops in her tracks. Her fearful face scans my body, and I remain still as they wander.

She's beautiful. Her skin a delicate cream, her slender body only covered with a large, holey, graphic T-shirt. The red hair on top of her head stands out even through the fog. My eyes travel to her bare, shapely legs.

I blink, remembering my purpose. Eliza, Jane's daughter. Her oncoming death, the blood, the horn . . . it passes through my mind like a movie on fast forward. My jaw flexes with the urge to protect her. She doesn't deserve for her life to end at such a young age. She doesn't deserve that kind of death, but it's one she'll have to endure. I can't stop it. I'm but a simple new shade. My only purpose is to cross her over just as Jane did for me.

Her eyes return to mine, confusion wrinkling her forehead, but curiosity swivels her head slightly to the left. The harsh edges of my eyes soften, sympathy panging inside my chest. My lips twitch as I fight the urge to tell her what all this means—the dream she's in, the fog, the place she'll die. She has no idea, just like I didn't.

Her eyes flick to my twitching lips before she shakes her head.

Thick, plump lips form words. "Who are you?" she whispers.

I stop ticking my jaw, tilt my head to the side, and part my lips slightly. Her voice, it's delicate . . . like a song. It stirs something inside me, something I never knew existed, and shocks me to my transparent core. It's a feeling I thought movies overplayed, yet here it is, consuming my insides like the fog around me.

Shoving away those thoughts, I consider how to answer her question without frightening her, without making her feel insane.

She starts hyperventilating. A few sharp intakes of breath, and her hands fly to her throat, fighting for air. I'm not sure if it's a real panic or if the lively fog is too thick for her to breathe. Or maybe it's the dream pulling her out?

My first time dreaming of Jane and the place of my death wasn't a frightening one. It felt so real, but I had convinced myself it wasn't. I remember that feeling of being pulled from our place of visit in that alley. It's like a rope tightening around your torso, tugging and pulling, cutting off the passage of air.

Sorrow fills my heart, and my eyebrows scrunch. Our time is coming to an end before it even starts. But . . . I know . . . I know without a doubt, I'll see her again. I swallow. I have no way to save her, no way to make it not happen.

I'm only a shade . . . a ghost.

It makes me question . . . who designs life, and who assigns death? And how do you stop that certain fate?

DYSON COLEMAN

THE TWEEN

Jane releases a sigh. Her breath gushes past her teeth, and her body sags with relief as Aiden crosses to bring back her daughter. I step back and place my hand on her shoulder, my lips tilting in my one-of-a-kind, sideways grin. Anything to ease her troubled heart. "Time works differently there. He'll be back before you know it."

The slight tendrils of fog sway this way and that, floating between our legs like it's another guest in our small group's rebellious mission. I suppose it is. It's the Reaper's Breath, its own entity.

Just like others from the Earth Realm, they say they could feel how cold Reaper's Breath was in their dreams. It surprised them that they could no longer feel the expected chill once they became a shade. It grows in the Tween, obscuring their view from taking in too much at one time. Each time they visit the Tween, Reaper's Breath shows a little more, easing the transition.

I see Jane nod, but my focus is on the swirls of cold I can no longer feel. It mimics that of the Death Realm. Its reason for being is not to provide warmth and comfort but preparation for the Death Realm itself.

The fog blends with our transparency, a marveling sight in such an area where beating hearts don't exist. As it licks my skin, it's hard to distinguish between where my body ends, and the fog begins.

I watch a second tendril float up the trunk of a tree, fitting in between the grooves of the jagged black bark, and slithering an indirect path of its own. The tree trunk is a solid structure, dark brown, while the fog is thick but transparent and white. Tangible density versus abstract sparsity. The color and consistency is such a striking contrast. Beautiful, almost.

It astonishes me how Reaper's Breath can be in many places at once, separating itself for any purpose it sees fit. But as each tendril goes about its own individual task, the Reaper's Breath is still one being, one mastermind.

I suppose that's a blessing, that there's always a piece of it floating close to Kheelan. If the creature were constantly gone, running its secret 'errands,' Kheelan would become suspicious, ending our plan before it can even begin.

Tanya sniffles. The sound breaks me from my thoughts, and I shift my head to her. "He'll be back," I repeat, my voice a mumble of distracted reassurance.

She tilts her head up. There isn't a sky in the Tween. The only thing visible is the fog and eerie, unmoving, dead branches.

She blinks away tears before returning her eyes to mine. "You're really a wolf-shifter?"

My lips tilt down and to the side in a sympathetic expression. I understand the reasoning behind her sudden change in subject. "Yep." I pop the 'p' like my old pack mate, Brenna, used to.

Sorrow rolls through me, gripping my chest like a vice, and momentarily consumes my thoughts before settling in the pit of my stomach like a heavy weight. I'll never see her again. Any of them. How am I supposed to find peace in death when life still haunts me?

It's not like I've had much of an adjustment. Heck, my wolf still barely acknowledges his existence, retreating to such a dark place that I'm finding myself forgetting he's even there. He's a ghost inside of a ghost.

"That's . . ." she pauses. Using the edge of her pointer finger, she catches the stray tear trickling down the slope of her cheek like a snake slinking across a desert sand. "I still don't know how I feel about all this."

Jane takes the few steps to her, folds her in a hug, and cradles her head on her shoulder. Her fingers fumble with Tanya's strands of hair as she shushes her. My throat constricts. It's two mothers finding comfort in the only way they can. I have no such luxuries.

"When did you die?" I mumble. I study the length of her body, looking for any signs of her demise.

Regrettably, I don't know Tanya well. Actually, I don't know any of the folks in the rebellion on a personal level, not to the extent that I should.

Every day, we discover new shades wanting to rebel against Kheelan and his unjust ruling. He and his vampires enjoy their little "games." Kheelan believes himself fit to do as he pleases, no matter who it affects or how. When you're as powerful as a Fee, it makes sense that it goes to your head.

We haven't figured out how to uproot him yet, but I imagine the root of the solution is related to the problem itself—the reason the realms are shifting, blurring. Something is bending the rules. I'm grateful for it, but that doesn't mean I don't want to find the cause. It's a tricky game we're playing, one that will surely come to a swift end. If I could find what's causing it, it stands to reason that maybe I could use it to my advantage.

Tanya lifts her head, glancing over Jane's shoulder. "A few weeks ago, maybe? Time passes so differently here. It could be longer." Jane pulls back from the hug. "I'm not sure."

"How did it happen?" Jane whispers.

Tanya blinks, her eyelashes dewy. "Heart complications during surgery."

Uncomfortable silence stretches on, none of us knowing how to comfort something that was destined to be.

I shuffle my feet, shifting my weight. "Look, we don't all need to wait here. You two head back. I'll wait for them." Jane turns around, opens her mouth to say something, but no words come out. "Maybe prepare their rooms? It may be best if they have a moment to adjust first."

Jane sighs and nods. "Come on, dear." She holds her hand out for Tanya. "Let's leave Dyson to it."

They give me one more look before glancing at the spot Aiden left. "Go on," I gently nudge.

Together, they walk in the direction Tanya and I traveled from. Back to the Death Realm, back to unjust treatments.

Once they're out of sight, I blow out a relieved sigh, my shoulders sagging from their uptight position. Grief had overtaken me when I said Brenna's favorite word. It consumed me. Swallowed me whole. Sending them away was more for me and less for them.

CHAPTER TWELVE

ELIZA PLAATS

THE TWEEN

Fog. White, misty fog. It swirls around my ankles, around my torso, around my head—smooth, thick curls, twirling themselves around me, welcoming me into its cold embrace.

My head swivels from side to side. My heart beats at a rapid pace. It's a flutter at first until I can feel it pound in my chest. I place a hand over my heart, ensuring it doesn't march through my ribcage.

Where am I?

I place a foot in front of me, and then another and another. My footfalls disturb the curls of fog, swirling it in new directions. It folds me in, seeps through my skin, my muscles, my bones. My stomach heaves.

A train track comes into view—a slight relief at the sight of such a familiar object.

"Hello?" I call out.

Nothing.

I turn around, my breaths coming in harsh gasps. Mist forms past my lips and mixes with the white fog, mingling and churning.

"Hel –" I stop. I see him. Someone's there. The fog parts, leaving a path.

Standing with his hands in the pockets of his jeans, a dark hooded sweatshirt conceals his face, and his feet bare, he remains a statue. Out of place. Too still to be real.

His face is tilted down. The hood from his sweater hides all but the bridge of his nose and the edge of his chin. He's broad, his sweater almost too small for his shoulders.

My eyes fall to his hips, to his thighs. I gulp, my heart thudding for a whole new reason. I recognize this man—that sweatshirt, those jeans, that build . . . I had just declared him dead.

I take a step forward, my legs shaking beneath me. I take another. A twig I can't see breaks beneath my bare foot.

"Hello?" I call, my voice barely above a whisper.

He tilts his head back, slowly at first, until his eyes meet mine. I gasp, his beauty strikes me, breaks my heart and puts it back together once more. I stop my advance. He's beautiful. Breathtaking. Innocence behind a steel mask. The dead man I saw in the E.R. is transformed, life seeming to fill his body, striking me to the very spot I stand. I had just mourned this stranger, and now here he is, in full view.

A square jaw, a straight nose, bright blue eyes that illuminate the fog around him. The blue pools so vivid, yet so void of life. I get lost in them, only for a moment, letting those almond-shaped spheres swallow me whole. He blinks, his long lashes brushing his cheekbone, and something in them transforms. The edges less harsh, curiosity or confusion replacing that steel.

Luscious red lips twitch, and my eyes flick to them, zoning in as my mind comes up with images and fantasies on its own accord. I shake my head, clearing the direction of my thoughts, and instead, marvel at the idea of him standing before me.

"Who are you?" I whisper.

His eyes soften at the sound of my voice. He tilts his head to the side, and his lips part slightly.

My breaths come in harsh gasps; my lungs force the air out without accepting passage for new oxygen to flow in. A weight, a construction forces itself around my rib cage. A fine sweat dribbles down my spine and my hands cup my throat as I fight to inhale.

I glance at him one more time. Such sorrow sketched in his brows, his mouth, the depths of those vivid blues. Stars speckle my vision, blooming to larger, bright circles before I'm pulled from the fog, and he fades with it.

****

I bolt upright in bed, clenching my sheets as if they're the only things holding me to Earth. My eyes fly open. My chest rises and falls. Images of my dream flash before me.

Where was I? The fog—that was no dream. I felt it. Even now, I still feel the chill of its swirls against my arms, raising the hairs on my body, peppering tiny bumps across my skin.

I push my hair back from my sweaty forehead, glancing at my sheets but seeing nothing except for him. I replay the encounter in my dream over and over. At the end, it seemed like he was going to say something. What was on the edge of that tongue?

He was a stranger, my dead patient, but I felt as though I've known him my whole life. Is this residual grief? My mind has to be playing tricks on me.

I climb out of bed, cross my room to the hallway, and enter the bathroom before flicking on the lights. I stare at myself in the mirror, both eyes searching the reasoning for such a dream. My messy red hair looks like a bird's nest.

What was that place? Where did my subconscious take me? Though I've trained my brain to work on the logical side of things—the scientific side—I refuse to accept that it was a dream. It felt so real.

Before the swirling fog, I was dreaming of my mom. It had been a memory of when I was young. She'd taken me to a field of flowers, and I'd pick them by the handfuls, just for her. She'd lift them to her nose and smile with delight. Such cherished memories, but my dreams taint them, taunt me, remind me of what I no longer have.

I turn on the faucet, check the temperature, and cup the flow in my hands. After splashing my face, my fingers fumble blindly for the hand towel before I grasp it and pat my face dry. I take a deep breath, look once more in the mirror at the lonely, broken person who dreams of mysteriously gorgeous and declared dead men, and flick off the light.

My footsteps are soft against the carpet as I walk through my dark apartment. I plop myself onto my leather couch and cover my legs with the plush throw blanket.

Snuggling into the cushion, I turn my head and stare blankly at my plain, white wall. No pictures hang there for me to gaze upon. My life is empty. No memories fill the four walls that hold the roof over my head. Could this be why I dream so vividly of the dead? After all, I can't help but compare my life to my deceased patient's. He had no one, just like me. Yes. Yes, this is the reason my mind played tricks on me.

In fluttered spurts, my eyelids rise and fall, each time a little more so than the last, until I'm plunged into sleep.

KATRIANE DUPONT

MYLA'S PAST

I follow Corbin down a tiny hallway to the first door on the right. The hallway is dark and narrow. No lights to brighten our path. I slide my hand along the wooden wall out of habit, a few slivers of wood breaking free against my fingertips. Corbin opens the door, the hinges creaking as he does so. "This was our bedroom," he explains. A charming grin crossing his lips, displaying impossibly white teeth. His eyes shine a bright green, making me pause in entering the dimly lit room.

I lean a little closer to his face. "Your eyes—they have color." Fee have pitch-black eyes. How does he not?

A chuckle rumbles inside his chest. "Glamour, little witch. Glamour."

Blinking, I roll my eyes under my lids. Of course it's glamour. How else would he fit into this realm?

Sniffing, I enter the small space that was once a bedroom shared between husband and wife. My finger trails along a large wooden chest with leather and brass décor riddled throughout before I turn back to him. "You don't seem sad about your wife's death."

A perfect eyebrow raises on his forehead. "Observant," he mumbles. He straightens his cape around his neck. "You are correct. I'm not upset."

My head cocks to the side, disbelief narrowing my eyes. "Why?"

His hand falls back to his side and he takes a step closer to me. He's intimidating. Perhaps it's because he controls the legends of nightmares, but his cocky attitude, his charming presence . . . it's as if he knows what makes a woman tick. That's frightening all on its own.

"What dies is never dead," he murmurs.

I blink a few times at him, questions forming in my head. "And you know this . . . how?" He shrugs, his lips tilting downward before the grin returns. "You enjoy mind-games, don't you?"

He laughs. It's throaty and musical all at once. "Yes," he answers simply.

"Well, let's not make me a game." I square my shoulders. "I plan to leave here, but I need a few items."

He cocks his head to the side. "Pray tell, what is your plan, daughter's daughter of my daughter?"

"Create a portal." I turn back to the chest, admiring the leather's detailed design, stroking it with my pointer finger and imagining what sort of tools they used to make such a masterpiece.

I look back at him. "Surely it can bring me back to my time period."

Shaking his head, he lowers his chin with each swipe to the side, glancing at me from under his lashes. "That won't work."

I cross my arms, kicking a foot out in a defiant stance. "And why not?"

His head jiggles at my flippant attitude. He's enjoying himself. "Two of you cannot be in the same time period. You must return to your body. It's impossible for you to return until the spell you're under is reversed."

My hands fall to my sides. "Spell? This is a spell?"

"Yes."

I bring a trembling hand to my lips. "By whom? Who would do such a thing?"

"The only one who is capable. Sureen." He crosses his arms.

Why would the Fee of the Dream Realm have any interest in me? I've never even met her. Is that why I was having dreams of Myla's memories? Did someone manipulate them? My eyes narrow as I come to one conclusion.

Right now, the only constant in my life is Tember, and she's constantly suspicious of my life and the secrets within it. If she was sent here for answers, she'd be bold enough to go digging herself.

A sandman manipulates dreams. If Tember convinced one to alter my sleeping state, chances are, Sureen found out about it and took her wrath out on me.

I should have never trusted an angel. I knew better.

"So, I could be stuck here forever?" I murmur.

Rocking back on his heels, he smirks. "Yes."

TEMBER

EARTH REALM

It's noon, and she has yet to move. At least she's breathing. Yes. She's alive.

There's only one thing left to do.

I walk to the living room. Pressure begins in my head, my eyes brightening as the halo forms around it. My vision is different this way. Minute details are visible—tiny mote specks, imperfections along Kat's skin, the specks of dirt hiding along the crevices of the bedroom wall spackle. I watch for a moment as my halo circles my head in slow motion, the sun coming through the window reflecting against it. It can't compete with the supernatural anomaly, bouncing off like it would a mirror and lighting the walls with a brilliant glow.

"Erma," I shout to the spackled ceiling of Kat's living room. My hair falls from my shoulders, tickling the small of my back. "Erma!" This is the only way angels can call our creator is if we show our true nature.

Wings or not, I still hold all the gifts bestowed upon me. I may not be able to return home, but I can still preform the Kiss, call upon Ire, my bow and arrow, and I can summon my maker. My wings were what made me who I am, but I'll be damned if I cower in a corner while my charge suffers a fate I know nothing about.

A glow of light—the same color as our halos, blindingly bright—forms in the middle of the living room. It's small at first until it grows, similar to Kat's portals. The air doesn't swirl or disturb, but every noise, no matter how small, is deafened.

Her foot is visible first before Erma walks through the portal like she's stepping down a flight of stairs. As soon as she's through the circle, it disappears, and the everyday life noises return. I find it a small and previously unnoticeable relief.

Erma glances around, bewildered, until her eyes rest on me. "Tember," she coos, a smile spreading across her beautiful face.

She holds out her arms, takes the few steps in my direction, and folds me into a lover's embrace. She's shorter than I and smells of sweet chocolate, just as I remembered. Though it's only been a few days, it feels like it's been years since I last held her.

I wrap my arms around her and kiss the top of her soft red hair. Breathing in her scent, I calm my emotionally raw and guilt-filled nerves.

Her fingers roam my back before she stiffens. "Tember . . . where are your wings?"

I freeze and swallow, the sound audible as my nervous energy returns. I hadn't thought of what her reaction would be once she found out and the excuse I'd give in return. She pulls back from our embrace, anger dipping her eyebrows toward her black eyes.

"I had to remove them. It was important to blend in."

Her eyes widen, and her lips part. "Tember, if you remove them, they don't grow back. You'll be stuck in Erline's Realm."

My toes curl inside my shoes, causing the skin to pinch along my feet. "I know."

Her fists clench and unclench. "You . . ." She looks me up and down, disbelief thick in her voice. "You sacrificed your wings—your home, me—to protect your charge?"

I square my shoulders and stiffen my neck. It seems I'm not the only one with selfish intentions. "Yes." My tone is even and not up for negotiations.

The deed is done. I sacrificed who I am, the very essence that makes me an angel, for the betterment of the realms. Kat is the betterment of the realms. I didn't realize how much until I selfishly inserted myself into her life, using her as a

186

tool. I became the sort of angel I despise, dipping my toes into the dark side.

"What have you done," she growls, her fists slamming to her sides.

I point at her, my eyes narrowing. "This is bigger than my wings, Erma. We have a problem."

Her face softens, but the steel is still etched across her eyes. "What could possibly be a bigger problem than the loss of your wings? Of your home? Of me?"

Hesitating, but refusing to back down, I keep my eyes focused on hers. "Myla."

She frowns, glancing at my torso. "Myla?" Her eyes return to mine. "Erline's daughter? What about her? She's dead."

I shake my head. "She isn't. Myla and Kat are one and the same."

Erma takes a step back, her anger disappearing, replaced with shock. "T-that can't be." She begins to stutter and glance around the room as if Myla herself will walk around the corner and unleash her almighty smite we've all heard about. "How?"

My body relaxes as the focus shifts from me to my charge. "Katriane made a deal with Erline to save her coven. Erline brought back her daughter's beast—the dragon. The dragon lives inside her and at points, takes over control. Though I'm not sure how true that is anymore."

Erma watches me for a moment, her mind working as quickly as the ticking of her jaw. "She would have had to keep her daughter's spirit from the Death Realm. Does she realize the consequence of that? Is this why Kheelan has left vampires here? They'll find her but not before they continue to wreak havoc on this town. Surely Kheelan has felt her return."

My head shifts as I glance away from Erma's gaze. "They already have," I mumble. "Myla and Kat destroyed them." I turn my head back to her. "That's not the only problem. The realms have shifted far more than we realized."

Erma sighs, her shoulders sagging in defeat. She walks over to the couch and gingerly sits on it like it's full of Earthly diseases. "Do tell."

"Her sandman. I asked him to replace Kat's dreams with Myla's memories." I sit down next to her.

Shifting her body to mine, her face remains calm though I know it's anything but. "Do you realize the consequences of that action?"

My voice lowers to a whisper, "I do now." I clear my throat. "He was feeling emotions, and it alerted Sureen. This last time, she came and retrieved her sandman, but not before she released her wrath."

Erma glares at me, shifting her body closer to mine in a challenging gesture. "Tember, you know how vengeful Sureen is. Do you have any idea what she's doing to her sandman right now? Do you know how she pulls the emotions from her creations?"

I hold up a hand, stopping her from going further with her chastising. "I'm sure I can imagine. That isn't the problem right now," I repeat, lowering my hand to my lap. My knowledge of Sureen and her realm is limited. "I can't wake Kat."

Erma's body remains still, her eyes unblinking, watching me as she connects the pieces. Her eyelids begin to squint in a glare, and she slowly stands, facing me with her full force of anger. "You should have consulted me on this, Tember. Sureen is known for her sleeping spells."

My face relaxes, and I take a deep breath. "So, she's just sleeping? Good. All we have to do is figure out how to wake her."

The growl that begins in her chest is so low and threatening it startles me. It would make a lion proud as it rumbles from her chest and spills out those perfectly plump red lips. Erma has never spoken to me this way. "You don't understand. Her spell sends the dreamer into a reality. Wherever Kat's dream is, that is where Kat is, in full corporal body."

I freeze, unblinking, staring at her with complete shock. My heart beats faster as my mind works to convince me that Erma's words are false. "I don't know where her dreams take her. I never asked Kat the exact location of her dreams – I was waiting to ask those questions until Kat worked them out herself. I never asked the sandman. I only instructed him to bring light to Myla's memories."

She lowers her torso, bending her hips and leaning toward me with menace. "Where ever it is, it's back in the 1600s when Myla was still alive. You've sent a witch back to the era when witch trials just began."

Gulping, my hand flies to my mouth, and I lean back into the couch with more force than necessary. My eyes wildly search the living room as if the shelves and furniture hold the answers I need. "What do we do?"

"Erline," Erma mumbles, but she's not talking to me. She's calling her fellow sister. They rarely do this—call upon each other. Fee cease to get along, which is why there isn't a realm full of them. They'd destroy it within minutes of being placed there.

Curls bounce as my head whips back to hers. Forceful winds pick up inside the tiny space of the apartment, announcing the incoming arrival of Erline.

CHAPTER THIRTEEN

DYSON COLEMAN

THE TWEEN

Leaning against the rough bark of a tree, I rub the back of my neck with stiff fingers. The pressure reminds me of my death. To have a rope painfully constricting around my neck, hung and dangling from a tree similar to the one against my back, and my lungs fighting for a sliver of air. I remember the rogue wolf-shifter's faces as they watched with wonder, like watching someone struggle for oxygen—for life—was the most fascinating thing of the century.

Their eyes were wide, unblinking, their lips parted in awe. I remember the burn of my lungs, the chafing of the thick, rough strands weaving the rope together. The black that consumed my vision, erasing all of my thoughts and feelings. Stealing my life. Their profiles are what I remember most, though. Every fine detail along their faces, every muscle tick under their skin. I remember wanting to beg, to shout at them, to plead for my life.

My mind drifts—my last goodbye to my best friend, Flint. I knew there was a chance I wouldn't make it back. I had mistakenly double crossed my Pack, my family, to save his life. Do they miss me? Am I worthy of being missed?

A thought crosses my mind, and I glance around before hesitating. I flex my jaw once before coming to a decision.

Bending to the dirt-covered ground, I hold out my hand. Nothing grows here, the trees are long since dead and brittle with disease that isn't immediately perceivable. This is the Tween. The place between life, and death. It seems fitting that neither life nor death has dominance here.

Reaper's Breath slithers to me along the dirt, reaching my fingertips before swirling up my arms, licking my transparent skin. It knows what I want—it always does. Just like Kheelan, it's able to read my thoughts, my desires, my hopes and dreams.

When Reaper's Breath had aided me before, it allowed me to bring some sort of peace to my soul. I had watched Flint destroy the one who had strung me. He had pushed the chair from under my feet and stood at my back as I struggled, my feet flailing, my nails digging at the rope, the blood trapped inside my face while every vein felt like it would burst. Zane felt nothing for my impending death. He was a willing slave to his leader.

Flint challenged Zane, avenging me even though I wasn't deserving of it. I was a traitor to my Pack . . . dishonorable. I had partially materialized, haunting Flint. He had seen me—our eyes had connected before he ripped the heart out of the enemy with his bare hand. But crossing like that— becoming partially manifested, haunting in the Earth's Realm— takes a lot out of a shade. To stay visible for long takes far more energy than we hold—those mere minutes left me weak for days.

I huff to myself. I don't regret it.

The fog expands up my arm before crossing my torso, swirling around my entire body in flowing waves. With no wind to direct Reaper's Breath, it's slightly unnerving. It's one thing to see fog, it's another thing to witness it move on its own. Even so, I know the creature means me no harm.

As it moves, I take a moment, remembering what it felt like to be human. A gentle breeze across bare skin, a ruffle of my hair. What my Pack smelled like. I let my mind bring up their images, their faces, their pitches of voice. Flint's goofy laugh flashes, and I hold onto the sound with desperation, remembering every detail of its tone. His face comes closer and closer in my mind's eye, and I dive into the memory of him. Relief floods me, momentarily taking over my grief.

It's working.

****

I find myself hovering, invisible, in the familiar woods I once roamed within the Cloven Pack's territory. This is home . . . was home.

A patch of trees is still missing—a tornado had torn through not too long ago, though it feels like it's been ages since. I was so angry back then, an emotion I'm presently regretting ever existed in my living soul. Life is too short; I know this now. It's a lesson I learned too late.

It's still dark—the early morning light has yet to show.

New trees are popping up through the soil, life blooming once more after devastation wiped the others from existence. I stare at it for a moment, knowing I won't be able to bend and touch it, to feel its silk run through my fingertips. To feel a callus on my palm snagging at the rivets. I'm not here. Even now, the breeze passes through me as if I'm nothing, nonexistent . . . nobody. This is simply a haunting, my shade's body left in the Tween to preserve energy. If I were to manifest, it'd take more energy than I have to spare.

As a being of the dead, it's the little things I miss. The comfort of home, the evidence of life—of a beating heart, a growing organism, a crisp smell, the hot baking sun. Everything was taken for granted when I could still breathe, when my heart still pounded within my chest.

A canine bark echoes ahead before it travels through the trees. I know that bark, I grew up with that bark. My wolf perks inside me, his ear tilting at attention.

Floating through the trees like a balloon directed by the wind, neatly trimmed grass spills into the clearing as I come to the edge of the forest. Flint's gray wolf is bent forward, swishing his tail from side to side as he teases Kenna's black wolf. Her wolf patiently waits, watching him bounce and prance before she strikes, tackling him to the thick grass. She's always been fast. It never ceases to amaze me.

I float beyond them to the stairs that climb the deck. Irene, Bre, and Victoria sit, chatting amongst themselves, mugs of tea littering the outdoor table.

Through the sliding glass door, I see Kelsey, her round, pregnant belly forcing her dining room chair away from the table.

Jeremy, her mate, grabs cookies lathered in pink frosting from a jar and places them in front of her. He kisses the top of her red-haired head while running his hand over her stomach.

A baby babbles in the blue highchair, his bright blond hair spiking in every direction as Evo feeds him yellow, mushy food with a blue, baby spoon. The baby opens his mouth like a new bird waiting for its mother to drop a slice of worm inside its mouth. His little arms wave in the air in anticipation for his next bite.

I watch them for a moment until parts of the women's conversation rips me from my sorrow.

"Whatever happened to Katriane? How is she doing these days?" Brenna askes Irene.

Irene shrugs underneath her large coat. I imagine this fall air is chilling. "I don't know. She hasn't been returning my calls."

Victoria shifts in her seat. "Remember that bonfire? Do you think what she said—about the Fee . . . Do you think it's all true?"

Scratching her cheek, Brenna answers, "It makes sense. She spoke of Erline—is that her name?" Irene nods. "She spoke of Erline like she knew her."

Shrugging again, Irene averts her gaze back to her mate playing on the grass with our Alpha female . . . their Alpha female. "She does. I just haven't gotten any answers from her yet."

Brenna bends forward. "You asked?"

"Of course I did." Irene crosses her ankles, grabs her mug, and takes a sip before setting it back down. "She won't tell me a thing. Kat is hiding something, and I intend to get answers. Someday, anyway."

The women are silent for a moment before Victoria speaks, "How involved do you think she is with the Fee?"

"Well," Brenna begins, "she did say that witches are Erline's daughters. I'm guessing she plays a big part with the world we never knew existed."

I tune out the conversation, my mind working frantically. Kat—Kat was the witch who conducted that mating ceremony last winter. Irene is a smart, educated woman. If she's suspicious of her, enough so that she isn't letting whatever Kat did go, it stands to reason that there's something more going on here.

If she's dabbling with the fee, could Katriane be the reason for the shift? It takes a powerful being to be such. Did she experiment with the dark? I don't know much about witches, but I imagine there are consequences for such things. It's worth investigating. For a moment, I find myself frustrated. How am I going to do any investigating in this realm if I'm stuck in the other?

The sliding glass door swings open, Evo stepping outside with a bundled-up baby wrapped in his arms.

"Coleman," Brenna coos, sticking out her arms to her brother, asking to hold the baby.

A ping hits my chest, filling it with consuming emotions. They named the baby after my last name.

Denial, anger, sorrow—it rips through me like a shredder, even though I know I have no right. They still love me. They named their baby after me. I'm loved. I'm missed. And I'm stuck, dead.

With practiced ease, I allow Reaper's Death to pull me back to the Tween, my living Pack mates disappearing in the swirling fog.

ELIZA PLAATS

THE TWEEN

My breath mists out in front of me, swirling and swaying in an unnatural, circular pattern. The fog is less dense, my vision clearer. I can now see the trees surrounding me, their sparse leaves blowing in the slight breeze, though I can only hear it.

There's a smell now. What is that smell? It's rich. Earthy. Spicy. I can't place it.

"Hello?" I call out, the word rushing across my tongue. I turn around, searching for him until my eyes land on the figure I just met.

He stands before the rails of the train, his hands in his pockets. This time he doesn't wait for me to call again before he lifts his head. His bright blue eyes shine a little brighter, his jaw less set—less hard.

Those baby blues search my face in a scorching slow motion, seeming to soak in every detail passed down from my mother and her mother before that. I tilt my head when his eyes land on my lips, his lips parting, but a breath of mist doesn't escape like mine does.

I take a step forward, and his eyes shoot back to mine, the hard, soulless stare seeing right through me. His lips close; his jaw ticks, the muscles rippling in his cheeks.

My mind flashes back to the corpse on my gurney. That muscle was dead, lifeless, no brain activity to construct its movements. But here he stands, a contradiction to the laws of life.

I dip my head and take another step. The smell grows stronger as I move closer. My breath comes in heavier spurts, the mist clouding my vision of him. I take another step. His body grows rigid as he eyes me carefully. The square jaw at the edge of his face angles when he shifts his head, speculating, considering, unsure.

One more step. I stand before him, taking him into my lungs, drinking in the aroma that's swirling around my head, up my nose, and licking my taste buds. My eyes flicker shut, savoring the flavor.

The lightest of touches brushes my cheek, stroking me in places I never knew existed. It heats my insides, fogs my thoughts, flutters my stomach, and fills my heart.

My lids twitch, but I keep them closed for fear I'll wake. This is but a dream. A lonely dream but still a dream. I keep them closed for fear it'll stop. I lean into it, and he pulls back a fraction. I freeze and squeeze my eyes, the skin wrinkling around the edges as I pray for his hand to return.

The pad of his thumb touches my lips, rubbing along the seam as he memorizes the texture. The breath I've been holding escapes, a relieved sigh. His skin brushes once more, and my shoulders relax, a sense of comfort and ease taking over. My reason for being returns, his skin scorching into mine, reminding *me who I am. Loneliness fades, replaced with a sense of belonging.*

His skin leaves mine, only to move to my chin. He grips it with soft but sure fingers, tilting my head back. I don't hear him shuffle forward, but I can feel him move closer. The slight vibrations of the breeze are now blocked by the man before me. I inhale, wanting one more taste.

Slowly, with an ease I've never had, I open my lids. I can only see his eyes as he towers above me. The blue depths are clearer, more intricate, as I search within them for the reason of all this, as if those very eyes hold the key to my questions.

Hunger, curiosity, wonder, float inside the still swirls of blue freckled with gray. He blinks, his lashes impossibly long. The sweet, delicious scent fans my face as he takes another careful breath.

His eyes flit back and forth between mine, his face carefully blank. He leans forward a fraction, searching my face, my eyes, my soul.

With tender ease, his eyes close as his lips brush against mine. Just one. Feather-like. Enough to make me want more.

I need more.

The heat in my lower abdomen is ablaze, swirling like the pits of hell with an insatiable need and an unquenchable desire. The thoughts in my mind are no longer heard. The flutters in my stomach an intense tickle. My heart pounding out of my chest, reminding me it beats. But his shouldn't.

Ignoring my sense of feeling so out of place, I move my lips against his as he brushes once more. Flicking out my tongue, I taste him. His hand reaches from my chin to my nape, tilting my head back and stroking the inside of my mouth. A gentle encounter, a careful massage.

I sigh and place my hand on his hips. His body tightens, ridged under my cautious fingers, his tongue pulling back into his mouth. He breaks the kiss and leans his forehead against mine. My eyelids flutter open and explore the man before me.

And I gasp.

I can see through him. He isn't real. He's . . . he's partially invisible.

Just as I'm lifting my hand to touch his cheek, to see if my fingers would slip through his flawless, transparent skin, he speaks. It caresses my insides, and my mouth parts once more as his breath fans over me. "It's time."

My eyebrows knit together. "Time for what?" He doesn't answer. He breathes me in before pain and anguish contort his angelic features. "Time for what?" I repeat.

With one hand, he pulls the string of his hood from its hole. He wads it up in his fingers and places the string in my palm, folding my hand around it.

His hand slips from my hair as I'm pulled away by an invisible force. "No. No, I don't want to wake." His hand remains, suspended in air, even after I'm a few feet away, before he stuffs his hands back into his pockets, watching me as I go against my will.

****

My eyelids flutter open, taking in the detail etched along my ceiling. A hot tear falls from my cheek. I touch my lips, the kiss still burning my delicate skin. Another tear falls, creating a straight trail down to the curve of my jaw.

I move my arm, my fingers twitching from their balled-up clench. Something smooth rubs against the inside of my palm, and I open my hand. Knitted cloth nestled within the cup of my palm. *What the hell is going on?*

CHAPTER FOURTEEN

KATRIANE DUPONT

MYLA'S PAST

Corbin lifts the lid of the wooden chest I ran my fingers along when I first entered the bedroom yesterday.

It's dark outside, another day gone. I've been cooped in this house while Corbin did who know's what and who knows where. He just came back as if he didn't abandon me, leaving me to fend for myself in a world I know nothing about. There's no food in this house, and my stomach growls it's protest. I don't know how to hunt, there's no fridge, no microwave. I feel small and insignificant here. I want my modern day comforts back. I want to leave this place.

Corbin crosses his arms over his chest. "These were Myla's dresses."

I sniff, glancing at the fine fabrics belonging only to this time period, eyeing them with disgust. I note there's nothing remotely black in here, and everything is a dress. I haven't worn a dress since my mother was the one who dressed me. "And what do you want me to do with them?"

He looks over his shoulder, his eyes wide with disbelief. "Wear them, of course. If you're going to be here, you must blend in. Get dressed, I'm taking you to eat."

"I'm not wearing that," I declare, backing up a step and curling my lip.

Taking a step toward me, he sneers, "You will."

We hold each other's eyes, neither wanting to back down, before my stomach growls so loud, his attention flicks to my abdomen.

Rolling my eyes, I take step toward the chest, careful to avoid him. Reluctantly, I pick up the first dress, examining the dark blue fabric and running it between my fingertips. "Won't they already know I'm not from here? It's a small village. Someone is bound to notice a newcomer."

He straightens his spine, the man with all the answers, while unfolding his arms to wave a large hand in the air. "Don't worry about such things. You're my niece." I turn my head, an eyebrow raised. "That's the story." His tone is final and not up for negotiations.

"Right," I state with sarcasm, my lip curling, before returning my eyes back to the dress. "And what do you plan to tell them about your disappearance before their eyes?"

"Simple," he says from behind me. "My wife was a witch who sent me to the woods."

I briefly shut my eyes, the memories of her death still haunting me, threatening to rip my soul from my body piece by piece. I wish I'd never come here, that I wasn't forced to witness it. I'll be damned if this goes unpunished when I return.

"Your eyes are glowing," Corbin says, humor in his tone.

ELIZA PLAATS

EARTH REALM

"Hey Eliza," Dr. Cassandra Grant greets me, her face and thoughts distracted, as I walk into the Attending's Lounge. Dark circles line her eyelids as if she hadn't had any sleep.

The room is empty, but the coffee pot has a fresh brew bubbling inside, filling the space with a pleasant aroma. My fellow surgeons will be trickling in soon, just to consume that coffee. If I plan to have a cup, I better do it now.

Cassandra glances up at me. "You look like crap. What the hell did you do last night?"

"Didn't sleep much," I grumble, hooking the strap of my purse inside my locker. I grab my lab coat and slip my arms through it.

She glances at me, eyeing me with speculation. She seems like she's about to say something, her mind working frantically, deciding if she should or not. Her eyes relax as soon as she comes to a decision, whatever that may be, and her lips twist before she speaks, "Look, I know losing your mother last year was rough, and that guy you couldn't revive . . . If you need to talk to someone . . ."

I wave off her unspoken request. "I'll be fine."

When my mom passed, she left me alone. I have no one left to call family. My job is consuming, leaving no room to date. I have no one. Nothing. The evidence of my lonely life is plastered on my face, the way I walk, the posture I hold myself in, the dreams my subconscious conjures, and the distance I keep from others.

The petite nose in the middle of her face usually wrinkles when she knows I'm lying, but today, she's distracted. For that, I'm grateful. "All right. But the offer is there if you ever need it."

I nod, turning my back on her as I grab my stethoscope and take a moment to breathe. I should ask her what's wrong, but right now, I'm selfishly consumed with myself. "Were you on call last night?"

"No, but I was called in."

I glance over my shoulder, seeing the fake smile on her mouth matching that of her falsely excited tone.

"There was a pile up on 5th and 7th. Shortly after I arrived home." She pauses and gulps. I almost ask her what's wrong, but I figure if she wanted me to know, she'd tell me. Right? "I was called to return. They said you had rough night and asked if I would take over for you. I've been in surgery most of the morning already."

"You should nap," I mutter, before turning my body to face her once more.

She stretches in her seat, lifting her arms over her head in a cat-like arch. The plastic chair squeaks, protesting the pressure against its back. "Nah. I have a few more good hours in me. Besides, we have surgery this morning."

I lift an eyebrow. "Mrs. Tiller still wants her Gastric Bypass?"

"Yep." Cassandra yawns. "You know what this means? You owe me that fifty bucks."

"There's still time for her to back out." I check the clock. "She has one hour left to change her mind. The bet has yet to unfold."

"I guess we'll see who's fifty bucks richer in an hour," Cassandra says. She grabs her lab coat off the chair next to her and stands.

****

I rip the wad of cash from my pocket and slap it in her hand as soon as we exit the scrub room. Mrs. Tiller indeed did have the surgery. But Mrs. Tiller never made it off the table. Her heart gave out. The monitor's flatline remains embedded in the back of my eyelids. The green line taunts me with every blink I make.

Fighting the lump in my throat, I scrub my face with my hands as Cassandra and I walk down the hall, the squeak of our sneakers against the tile louder than usual. She grabs my shoulder and stops me, tilting me to face her.

"I can tell the family," she mumbles, her eyes wet with unshed tears. "Why don't you get some rest? You don't look so good."

My jaw ticks, and I fight with the words that want to lash off my tongue. I bite them back, chanting to myself that this isn't anyone's fault. Death happens, and we can never predict when it will. This is a lesson I'm well versed in.

My first death has haunted me since it happened. Her name was Tanya, and she was alone, just like me, just like the dead man that plagues my dreams. I never forget a death, and it never gets easier to deal with. Her heart gave out during a routine surgery.

I give a curt nod. Her eyes travel my face once more before bringing me into a warm embrace. Her hands leave before I'm ready to let go of her, and she heads down the hall, her sneakers leaving black smudges against the white tile. I watch her walk away, her shoulders sagging as she deals with her own emotions, her own grief.

I sigh and swallow my tears, heading to the nearest on-call room. Opening the door, I kick it shut with my foot and rest my back against it, closing my eyes. To my relief, the room is empty, the beds vacant.

My head thumps against the door, and I rip off my scrub cap. My fingers tremble, and my throat constricts as it desperately tries to dispel the cemented lump threatening to choke me. Anger, grief, guilt, sorrow . . . they rip through my body without my consent, tumbling within my heart before spilling down each limb. She's gone. She no longer exists. Her spirit—her soul—never to walk this planet again. Just like *him.*

Taking deep breaths, I concentrate on the flow of air moving in and out of my lungs. The sound it makes, the feel as it travels, the rise and fall of my chest.

A familiar spicy, earthy scent trickles into the room, subtle at first before it grows and pulls me from my concentration. My nostrils flare as I inhale, the scent swirling in the pit of my grief-stricken, tight lungs, treasuring the aroma.

He's here. *That's not possible.*

And that's when I feel him. I tense when an invisible hand cups my cheek, and a thumb brushes my tear away. My heart thuds, his touch easing the crippling emotions that are settled there. I open my eyes, but nothing is there.

209

The other hand settles over my other cheek, rubbing a thumb back and forth over my cheekbone. My eyes flutter shut, letting his breath fan over my face, soaking into my pores. He's so near I can almost taste him.

What is he? Why can't I see him? Is he real? Am I losing my mind?

As a doctor, I know hallucinations come with a variety of illnesses. Is this what that is? But what about the string from his sweatshirt. How did that come into my possession?

Something brushes my nose. His nose? The scent fans my lips, and I open my mouth, consuming him, embedding him in my soul. A sense of calm replaces my sorrow, his presence the only song my heart beats to.

One more brush of a newly fallen tear, and the touch—my anchor—leaves. The dam breaks, the flow of moisture from my eyes replaces the point where his invisible hands once were. I slide down the door and sink to the floor, sobs wracking my body.

DYSON COLEMAN

THE TWEEN

My body shakes as I return. The feeling of reentering my shade's form is unsettling and draining. I draw in an unnecessary breath and quickly open my eyes. The conversation I just heard about Kat is a revelation itself. It leaves me to question what she is, but I'm without a doubt certain that she's the reason for the shift. I've never believed in coincidences.

Reaper's Breath hovers in front of my face, its tendrils urgently stroking my cheek, pushing my face—a warning. I glance around, searching for reason for it.

There, off in the distance, a hooded, cloaked figure floats across the forest floor, hovering inches above the dirt. Its face completely concealed as if nothing is there to begin with.

In a haste, I move to the side of the tree, concealing myself from view. I lean my head against the bark, closing my eyes and flattening myself further against it, before shifting ever so slightly to catch a glimpse. If I'm caught by a reaper, it'll surely be the end of me and my rebellion.

The forest is silent, Reaper's Breath hovering over my shoulder as I remain as still as possible. As soon as the edge of a black cloak comes into my peripheral vision, I shimmy over, using the tree to keep me hidden.

The reaper pauses its step, and if I were to have a beating heart, it would have surely stopped. Reaper's Breath freezes beside me, coming to the same conclusion that the reaper senses me.

As the reaper shifts, Reaper's Breath swirls around me, beginning at my head and working its way to my feet so fast that I barely register what's happening until I'm completely invisible.

I glance back at the reaper, its black hood tilted in my direction. Ragged breaths leave the creature, its face hidden. Even with it so close, I can't make out any details of its face. It it weren't for the breaths leaving the creature, I'd believe it was only a floating hooded cloak that stands before me. Its wide shoulders rise and fall with each inhale and exhale. The movement is so exaggerated, so creepy, it it makes me gulp.

The reaper lingers for a moment, the hood slightly shifting from side to side as it scans the forest for me, before turning its head back to its path.

As it floats by, I catch a glimpse of the shade following it. It's a plump older woman, a frightened look on her face as she follows the creature with no soul. She glances around the forest, taking in her surroundings. Even from here, I can tell she's unwilling, hesitant to keep taking those steps forward.

I wonder what Kheelan will have in store for this one. I shudder at the thought.

Erma tells Erline the entire story, and together, they stand in front of me like parents reprimanding their unruly adolescent. I shrink back into the couch, my resolve faltering under the gaze of these two powerful beings.

Erma glances at Erline. "Can you find her?"

Erline's jaw ticks as she continues to glare at me. Her long blond—almost white—hair cascades down her shoulders and back, blending with her flowing, moving dress and her pale, alabaster skin. "No."

Pacing the floor, Erma curses in a language I've never heard before, turning to face Erline's back. "Tell us what you know."

Erline straightens and slowly swivels her body, angling it toward Erma. "I know everything that crosses my realm. Every being, every creature that isn't my creation—I know when they're here."

She pauses, and my impatience grows thin. "And?"

Her head whips back to me, a snarl curling her lip for speaking out of turn. "Shades are crossing over, collecting the dead in place of the reapers. A few months back, Kat assisted in destroying a horde of vampires on shifter territory. A member of their Pack was found dead, and Kat used Myla's magic to find who was responsible. He was the first to cross over, the first to haunt this realm since Myla was alive."

Erma crosses her arms. "The realms are shifting more than I realized."

"Yes," Erline answers, softening her gaze before she turns it back to her Fee sister. "If your thoughts are accurate, and the sandman connected to Kat is indeed feeling emotions, it's likely all the realms have shifted because of her connection to each creature." She glances back at me. "Has anything else happened?"

I chew the inside of my lip, going over the last few days I've spent with Kat. "Corbin," I whisper. "She saw Corbin."

Erline's shoulders sag. "It was only a matter of time. They're connected, bound by my magic."

"How?" Erma asks.

A sigh escapes Erline's perfect lips. "In Myla's first life, Corbin found her and threatened to expose her whereabouts to Kheelan. He swore he wouldn't if I allowed a union."

I frown, my chin tucking slightly. I hadn't taken Kat seriously when she said as much. "A marriage?"

Erline nods. "They had two daughters, beginning the era of the witches." She frowns, her lips forming a hard line. "You said there's been an increase in vampires?" I nod, my curls bouncing and brushing my cheeks. "That explains the outbreak of a new flu virus."

My eyes close briefly. "It's not the flu, is it? It's the side effects from a vampire feeding."

"Correct," she answers, her tone flat. "Kheelan knows she's here."

"I don't understand," Erma begins. "When Myla died, didn't she travel to the Death Realm?" Her voice is thick with sarcasm. She already knows the answer.

Erline draws in a breath, her head tilting toward the ceiling. "No. I stole her spirit."

"Erline," Erma breathes in disbelief, her eyes growing wide. "You planned this? You planned the resurrection of your daughter?"

She doesn't answer Erma's question.

Erma's voice dips, her words full of anger. "You planned this, didn't you? What about the Red Death? Did you know a witch would beg for help? Did you bring that disease?"

"No," Erline whispers. "Kheelan did. It was his last attempt to flush out Myla. Since she didn't arrive in his realm, he knew she was still here with me. His vampires weren't aiding him as well as he'd like, so he sent the disease."

Erma contemplates, her Adam's apple bobbing as she swallows. "Why did you bring her back, Erline? Why did you keep her spirit?"

"So no one else could have her."

"You used the Red Death," Erma whispers. "You used it. You knew a witch would come to you – would beg you – and you used it to your advantage. And for what? To bring back your daughter? To threaten the realms? Everyone is in jeopardy because of you. Myla – her beast – is powerful, Erline. More powerful than you or me. And now it's in the hands of a witch who has no control over it."

"What do we do?" I ask, changing the subject before the Fee unleash their wrath upon each other. This apartment isn't the right size for a miniature Fee war, and an angel with no wings isn't enough to stop them.

Looking back to me, Erline's eyes grow soft in defeat. "We need Corbin. We need her location, and he's the only one who would be privy to that information."

CHAPTER FIFTEEN

ELIZA PLAATS

EARTH REALM

I brush my teeth more eagerly than the previous times in my life. In a few short minutes, I'll be asleep. I'll be with him.

With nervous energy, I glance at the ball of string beside my sink. I have no doubt he's already there, standing in the fog, searching the empty space by the train tracks, waiting for me to appear. With no clue to who he is, I'm resolved to get answers. Why does he haunt me? I brush faster, spit, and rinse my mouth.

I shouldn't feed my subconscious' lunatic thoughts. What is happening to me is completely impossible. If this were real, it would go against every scientific fact known to mankind. Yet, I can't stop myself from believing it's all real—all true.

Crossing the hall to my bedroom, I flick off the lights and climb under my comforter, my sheets cold against my bare legs. My large shirt bunches around my waist, and my head sinks into the pillow, my eyes on the white ceiling. Under the blankets, my toes wiggle with impatience. *Come on, Eliza. Fall asleep.*

I begin counting non-existent sheep. *One . . . two . . . three . . .* I don't know what number I reach, but it doesn't matter. Sleep descends, and with it, my heart sings only for him.

****

Vivid. That's the first thing that comes to mind. Everything is so vivid. There's no fog. I can see the tops of the trees blowing in the slight breeze. They wave and sway, a dance of their own. The way this dream feels so lucid fascinates me.

Trees are everywhere, fallen logs and limbs at their bases. Dead leaves in a variety of colors crunch under the soles of my feet as I shift to get a better view. This place looks so familiar, and my eyebrows knit together as I try to remember.

These are the tracks I travel over when driving across the bridge before I reach the edge of the city. Yes, that's it!

Train tracks part the trees, and my purpose for being here comes into the forefront of my mind. I turn so fast I almost lose my balance, desperate just to see him—anxious to touch him, concerned he may not be waiting.

218

But there he is, his hands at his sides, hood removed . . . and my eyes catch his. He stands before the track's curve around the trees, feet side by side. A small smile lights his transparent face—the face of an angel.

He shifts his weight a little, tilts his head to the side and blinks.

Dark, unruly hair waves in every direction. The tousled look makes him real.

My heart skips a beat.

He's dressed in his sweatshirt and blue jeans, just like before. Without the dense, unnatural fog, I faintly see the scene behind him, right through his skin.

My heart skips another beat . . .

I smile and dig my bare feet into the ground. I run for him, my arms propel my steps. His arms wrap around my waist before mine wrap around his neck. My face buries under his jaw, and I breathe deep, smiling against his skin as my eyelids flutter shut and skim the surface of his translucent skin. He rubs his cheek against my neck, holding me in his arms while he waits for me.

He knows. He knows he's my anchor.

I lift my head, my lips searching for his. He responds easily, the hard edge gone, and I think . . . maybe, just maybe, I'm his anchor, too.

Did I pull him from his inner darkness as he did for me?

219

A stroke of tongue.

Am I what he waits for?

A brush of lips.

Do I remind him of who he is?

I run my hand through his hair, feeling its coarse texture through my fingertips. He lifts me up, though I don't know how. How am I even touching him when I can see through him?

I tilt my head, deepening the kiss. Another stroke, another touch, his taste igniting a blaze.

He walks a short distance, his feet never rustling the leaves, never snapping the twigs, before he stops and places me on a fallen log just off the train tracks. Leaning me back against the bark, he doesn't break the kiss as he settles between my thighs, overtop of me. His jeans brush against the woven threads of my underwear. The back of my bare legs scrape against the rough edges of the fallen tree, enticing a new level of pleasure.

His hands travel up my leg, skimming the top of my underwear and under my shirt. It's slow, agonizing. It's too fast, not fast enough. My stomach dips at the sensitive touch, and he splays his hands across it. His tongue dives in again, slow and gentle just like his trace against my abdomen. Loving. Caressing. One thousand words in one touch. One thousand emotions.

The fingers travel further to my rib cage, to the swell of my breast. I sigh into his mouth as his fingers brush against my nipple. Heat travels from my peaks to my core, and I shiver. My hand grips the back of his hair, gently running through the short strands.

For a brief moment, my subconscious screams at me that this isn't real, that I shouldn't be able to touch something unless it's tangible. But here I am, doing so, feeling his body with my own touch, with my own nervous system. I squash my subconscious' voice like a pesky bug beneath my foot.

He brushes my nipple again, and my hips thrust against his. I feel his erection from inside his jeans, and I apply more pressure. Wanting more, needing more, while knowing this shouldn't be real. He bites my bottom lip, and our eyes open at the same time. Such heat, such passion, such . . . love.

The blue eyes drink me in, searching my face, memorizing it. I brush his swollen lip with my pointer finger, testing my own theories, and he closes his eyes. Taking a deep breath, his chest presses against mine on the inhale. He opens his eyes again, determination now within their pools, his jaw set.

Removing his hand from my breast, he traces down the same path he entered, down to the rim of my underwear. The trail is deliberate, warm, leaving goosebumps in its wake. He watches me, tilting his head, as he carefully removes the thin cloth. His tongue slides out, licking his bottom lip, leaving moisture there. His body's pressure briefly leaves mine, and he pulls my underwear the rest of the way down, dropping them to the leaves.

Unbuttoning his jeans, he lowers himself back overtop me. I hear his fingers lower his zipper as his lips massage my *collarbone. Small pecking sounds reach my ears with each carefully placed kiss.*

I inhale the scent of his hair, my eyes opening and shutting in slow waves. My heart fills, my body whole, and I feel everything. Every stroke of his lips, every swirling breeze against my exposed skin. I've never felt so alive.

He lifts his bottom a tad, lowering his jeans, before settling between my legs once more. I suck in a breath, his erection against my most intimate parts. He lifts his head, searches my eyes, and places a kiss to each lid.

I open my legs a fraction wider, gesturing acceptance. I want this—I need this. I bite my bottom lip.

He stills his movements before dipping his hips and pressing his tip against my folds. Pausing, he waits for me to object. I open my legs just a little more and brush my bottom lip against his chin, a kiss on his jaw, and lastly, a nibble on the dip above his collarbone.

Pressure, wondrous pressure, parts my folds as he slides in. My walls stretch and flex, letting him fully sheathe, as if my body knows he belongs just as my heart does, subconscious be damned. He belongs in the chambers of that once broken and lifeless heart.

My head rests against the bark. My back arches, my breasts press against his chest, and a soft sigh escapes my open mouth. He lowers his head, running his lips against my jaw bone before pulling back and sliding in. I gasp, every sensation felt. His breath fans my neck as his nose nudges the crook.

He pulls back out and slides back in. My fingers grip his hoody, fumbling for skin. He lifts himself up and removes it, tousling his hair in a new array as it slides over his head. My eyes greedily run over his body and land over the inch-sized slice marring the skin on his chest, just over where his heart is. Its edges jagged, rough. Foreign. It's exactly what I saw in the E.R. room. It still looks so fresh, unhealed, but no blood seeps from the wound. I feel my subconscious gain ground—that this isn't possible. I run my fingers over it, recognizing it for what it is.

My eyes lift to his, questioning, my brain at war with my heart. Is he alive? Am I alive? Is this just a dream?

His eyes close slowly, a silent gesture that he's well. He grabs my hand from skimming his wound and brings it to his lips, watching me as he places a gentle, sensual kiss to the palm. Lowering himself over my body once more, those same lips capture mine.

He continues his pumps, and a soft moan rumbles up my throat and out my mouth, fanning his and my face. His nose brushes against mine, an affectionate touch.

The heat builds and tugs, slowly at first. My back arches against the bark. My stomach presses against his. He lowers his face and breathes on my neck. His inhales and exhales long, tickling my ears, the evidence of his own pleasure matching that of my own.

He lifts my shirt, our skin brushing against each other as he rocks to the rhythm of my heart. A soft moan vibrates his chest, tickling my peaks. I capture it with my mouth, savoring the moment, the flavor, taking his pleasure and adding it to my own.

The heat in my lower abdomen raises—a pressure now confined in a bubble that threatens to burst.

He shifts his body and his teeth graze my shoulder. My pants harsh, the stroke of teeth sending me over the edge, and the bubble bursts.

My legs quiver and wrap around his hips. He rides my waves of pleasure, my walls clamping around his shaft in mild strokes. He groans, his lips replacing his teeth, easing the slight ache. Two quick pumps and he stills his movements. Small, breathy grunts skim my skin, swirling around my nose, tickling my taste buds.

Leaning his head against mine, he waits for the pleasure to subside. I run my fingers over his back, feeling the ripple of muscle, the dip of his hips, the curve of his shoulder blades. He shivers under my touch.

But I can still see through him.

"What is this?" I whisper.

He doesn't move, doesn't give any indication that he's heard me.

"What are you?" I ask a little louder.

He waits for a few beats of my heart before he answers, "I'm here with you. That's all that matters."

I shift under his weight, and he pulls his forehead back from mine, locking eyes.

"But you're dead. I called your time of death," I whisper, getting lost in those baby blue traps.

He tucks a strand of hair behind my ear, his fingers tracing the rim. "I am," he mumbles.

"Eliza," I introduce myself.

Sorrow takes over his features; his lids lower, and his eyebrows knit together. "I know," he mumbles.

"How do you—" I begin to ask before I feel the pulling sensation. "No. No. NO. I'm not ready to leave."

Pain crosses his face. My time is over here. He doesn't want me to leave any more than I do.

I panic. "How do I stay?"

He searches my eyes with his grief-stricken ones before lowering his head, placing a kiss on my lips. The kiss is full of everything he doesn't, can't, or won't say. It's soft, but firm, sinking from the skin to the bottom of my toes. My heart fills one last time . . . and I'm gone.

CHAPTER SIXTEEN

KATRIANE DUPONT

MYLA'S PAST

"So, this is what's considered 'fun' in the 1600s?" I ask, planting my dress-covered rump on a chair inside the tavern.

Everything is wood—from the posts supporting the ceiling to the walls. No décor besides the occasional cobweb littering the beams, no special touches besides the notches along the table—made from knives, no doubt. A few rooms are off to the side, and my imagination runs wild with what's happening behind those doors. This isn't a time period where sex is discussed.

"Keep your voice down or someone will hear you," Corbin mumbles.

I grab my ale placed on the table before me and take a sip. My mouth splutters with the unexpected sour brew. I set it back down, eyeing it with disgust. "Maybe if they hang me, I'll return to my time, in my own body."

He glares at me, showing a true emotion, not masked with intimidation. "No. If you die you will travel to the Death Realm, and your body back in your time will die."

I blink at him. "Lovely," I mumble. I pick up my ale, and before I take another sip, I stop myself, setting it back on the table.

"You don't like it?" he asks with humor, eyeing my drink.

"It's disgusting. I'm surprised you're all still alive after drinking that stuff. I'm almost positive it's piss."

He smirks and takes a sip of his own. "Women aren't allowed to speak like that here. I must say, it's refreshing."

I humph and glance around the bar. Men sing off in a corner, a celebration of the dead witch, no doubt. A man, holding the hand of a giggling woman, heads into one of the rooms.

"See something you like?" Corbin asks, returning my focus back to him.

"Hardly," I reply with a sneer.

He leans closer to me, his scent swirling around the space and clogging my thoughts for a moment. My coherent subconscious screams at me to lean away, but I hold my ground. I won't let his natural charm deter me. He's a relative for goodness sakes.

Corbin smirks, clearly privy to my inner turmoil. "Are you positive?"

My jaw ticks, and my hands clasped in my lap tighten around each other. "Your wife is dead," I remind him through clenched teeth. "You're my relative."

He leans away, resting his back against the wooden chair. "So you keep telling me."

"Have you no soul?" I growl.

Blinking innocently, he replies with a simple answer that sends goosebumps across my arms. "No."

A wave of lust hits me square in the chest. It frightens and disgusts me at the same time. My attraction to him is undeniable, and frankly, misplaced. It's as if my body is being manipulated, heating my core with desire. "Stop it," I snarl.

He grins, his sparkling teeth causing my eyes to shift to them. I watch his lips slide over their surface, mesmerized as he speaks one word. "No."

A shiver runs up my spine, and my fingers pinch themselves harder. My muscles grow ridged as I fight the unnatural lust. He's doing this. He's just like his creations – manipulating with promises not meant to be kept and a level of intimidation reserved for superiors. Maybe I frighten him, so he feels the need gain the ground.

"Is this how you won your wife over?" I mutter, my eyes on his plump lips.

They part, beginning to form words, before he's distracted by a scream just outside. The patrons of the bar don't hear it, but it's just enough to distract him and give me a breather.

I take a deep breath before turning my attention to the scream. "What was that?"

He looks back at me, picks up his drink distractedly, and takes a sip. "Most likely nothing."

My eyes narrow at him, the heartless ass, and I slide my chair back, standing. I intend to show him what compassion looks like as I march toward the door to the outside world.

"Kat, wait," he begins before I hear the scrape of his chair being slid back.

I move faster and exit the door. The chill of the night briefly bites my skin as I look left to right. The circle of the town is abandoned, the citizens either intoxicated beyond repair or tucked safely in their beds as if taking a life has set this town at ease.

The scream echoes louder out here, off to my right. My head whips in that direction, and my feet begin to move. I lift my heavy dress slightly, giving my feet more room to take wider steps.

Rounding the corner of the tavern, I come face to face with the source of the scream. A man has a plump, scarcely dressed woman pressed against the wall. His hands roam her body as she struggles, his face in the crook of her neck.

"Hey!" I shout, taking a few steps forward. "Leave her be!"

He doesn't listen to me, and my anger skyrockets. My hatred for the man roars through my body, adrenaline causing my thoughts to focus on bad choices. I place my hand on his shoulder and pull him off her.

He staggers, clearly intoxicated, before his wandering eyes find mine. They widen in fear, and for a moment, I ponder why that might be until I notice the glow from my eyes lighting his skin in a pale orange color.

"Witch!" he yells, staggering back a few steps. "Witch!"

ELIZA PLAATS

EARTH REALM

What is this? Am I going insane? Am I sick?

The windshield wipers briefly cross my view as they slide the water from one end to the other. The rain is heavy, pounding the pavement and flowing into ditches.

I'm late for my evening shift, spending most of my day pacing my floor. I'm going insane. I had sex in a dream, waking with the evidence of it in my underwear. This can't be real. That can't be real. He can't be real.

Can he?

No. He's dead, my subconscious growls.

I come to a stop just before the one-lane bridge. My wipers work frantically to keep up with the downpour. The tropical storm has been going on for days now, with no end in sight. I squint my eyes, checking for oncoming traffic, but it's nearly impossible to see beyond my windshield. I chance it, my mind consumed with my thoughts of the dead man who holds my heart. The man who can't possibly be real. I drive forward, pressing my foot on the gas and continuing my way to work.

Lights on my driver-side window blind my eyes. My head spins to the side. A gasp doesn't have time to leave my lungs before the lights connect with my car, a crunch so loud to my ears that they ring.

Metal scrapes against metal.

Windows break.

Glass flies.

My head whips to the side.

Pain shoots down my neck.

Hair blocks my vision.

I briefly hear a crunch to the other side of my car before I feel it topple over the bridge. Grabbing my steering wheel, the glassless windshield my only view, I watch in slow motion as glass and the contents of my car float around the open space. The shades of brown, dead leaves, and the train tracks come into my view as I draw nearer to the ground.

Slow sounds, slow motions, my car's roof crunches into the metal of the tracks. My head bangs against the roof from the force of impact. I hear a crack inside me, a brief moment of pain, before my legs tingle and go numb.

Blackness comes and goes. I groan, but I can't hear it.

Another set of lights shine through my car, and I glance at it from the corner of my eye, suspended upside down, held prisoner by my seatbelt. I try to tilt my head, but it doesn't move—like it doesn't belong to my body, as if it isn't under the control of my brain.

A train's horn reaches my near-deaf ears, and my eyes grow wide. My brain instructs my fingers to unclick my seatbelt—to flee—but my hands dangle. My fingers brush against the roof of the car, the life gone from them.

Heart thudding in an odd rhythm, fear spiking through my bloodstream, the train continues forward. Time speeds up and then slows down when my fearful eyes flick to a figure off to the side.

He is standing there, a few feet from my car. My Aiden. The keeper of my heart.

His hands are in his pockets, his hood pulled over his head, and he watches me, frozen in place. I see a tear drop from his chin and mix with the rain. I want to plead with him, to ask him to save me, but the words refuse to leave my mouth. All that passes my lips are gargled noises, blood foaming at the sides and dribbling up my cheek.

The train's horn sounds once more, and I glance again at the lights. I gasp, squeeze my eyes shut, and the train hits.

****

I float through the floor of my car, my body flying and soaring above it. The wheels still spin, the bottom of the car smoking in its crumpled heap.

The rain pounds the ground, the surface of everything it touches except for me. I glance at my hands as my feet settle on the wet leaves. They're see-through. I stare at them in wonder before my eyes lift to him, to my Aiden.

I am what he is. Dead.

He lowers the hood off his head, one hand still in his pocket. Behind him, our tree, our log. Our spot.

My heart doesn't beat, but something else fills the place as I get lost in his blue eyes. He holds out his hand.

"You came for me," I whisper.

He dips his head. He blinks. Tears stream down his face. "I came for you."

I take a step forward.

He's a ghost. I'm a ghost.

Another step closer. He came for me. For me.

Another step, and I grab his outstretched hand.

He looks down at me, a small, sad smile breaking the corners of his mouth. Reality sets in, and I glance once more at the wreckage.

"Why did you come for me?" I whisper.

He's silent for a moment, his voice rumbling behind me, thick from unshed tears. "I didn't—I- I was sent for you."

Taking the first step toward the tree line, he squeezes my hand once. I tear my eyes from my lifeless body and glance back up at him. He leans in, brushes my cheek with the pad of his thumb, and kisses my lips.

"Come on," he murmurs.

I follow him. My love. The keeper of my heart. My feet no longer crunch the leaves and twigs. The raindrops don't pound my skin, soak my clothes.

My ghost, my shade, one step behind him . . . we fade.

CHAPTER SEVENTEEN

TEMBER

EARTH REALM

Corbin arrives in a blink. One moment there's nothing there, the next, he's standing before us. A toothy grin spreads across his face, and his eyes hold anything but a welcome expression.

"You beckoned?" he asks taking a bow.

Erline growls, "Stand up, you fool."

If it were possible, I'd imagine his grin would spread wider.

Corbin rights himself and glances around the room. "Ahh, the home of my wife." His eyes land on Erline. His smile disappears, and malice replaces it as he stares her down. "The wife you failed to mention returned to a body."

Erline's fingers ball into fists, losing her facade of relaxation. "She isn't your wife anymore. The union broke at death."

His lips thin, and he takes a step forward. "We'll see about that."

"Enough!" Erma yells. Our attention turns to her.

She quickly tells the tale of our current predicament. Corbin's face remains blank, impassive, as he listens.

When she finishes, his head slowly turns to me. Once again, the blame falls on my shoulders. "This is your doing," he growls. The blank expression frightens me.

Corbin is a powerful Fee, almost more so than Erma and Erline. His specialty is fear and manipulation, creating creatures that enforce it. The more innocent the victim, the better they succeed, the more they feed. It is what sustains them.

Though that fear tenses my muscles, I ignore it, standing from the couch with ease, and look him straight in the eye. "What's done is done. How do we fix it?"

He cocks his head to the side. "I have memories that have been resurfacing. Some new, some old. Kat is indeed in the sixteenth century, living inside my home."

Erma takes a step forward, her eyebrows dipping. "You're just now telling us this?"

Corbin shrugs as if it means nothing to him. "I owe you nothing."

"How do we fix it?" I repeat before anything else can be said.

"It's simple," he says, cocking his head to the side while a handsome, charming smile lifts his cheeks. "I believe it's time to pay a visit to Sureen." He rocks on the backs of his heels, glee making him giddy. "Who wishes to provide transportation for our little rescue adventure?"

DYSON COLEMAN

THE TWEEN

Reaper's Breath returns me to visibility. I shake my head, swallowing back every emotion that's threatening to consume me while desperately trying to revise my plan, inserting the witch into the fold. At some point, I'll need to hold a two-sided conversation with her. I'll grovel if I must. Millions of shades depend on the usurping of Kheelan, including the woman who just passed me by.

When I hear quiet chatting, my eyelids fly open, my head swiveling in the direction the noise comes from, worried it's another reaper.

Aiden holds the hand of a female, Eliza. She whispers questions to him as they leisurely stroll through the lifeless forest. I watch her and the habit of picking up her feet to avoid the fallen branches, whereas Aiden has already caught on, letting his transparent body pass right through the wood.

He pauses, turning his body toward hers. I can't see his face anymore, but I can see hers through the back of his head. Her eyes flit between his eyes before he leans forward, brushing his lips against hers.

It's a tender kiss, one rarely seen. The sort of affection and love that's been extinct for years.

His fingers slide through her hair while her eyelids flutter, and her shoulders sag. He brushes her cheek with his thumb, and she smiles at him before they turn, continuing their walk.

Their steps are light, careless, like they're taking a leisurely stroll in a friendly neighborhood on a beautiful sunny day. As if they have all the time in the world.

As they get closer, Aiden catches my eye and points. "There he is," he says, wrapping his arm around Eliza's waist. "It's Dyson, right?"

I nod absentmindedly, my eyes glued to his arm and the fingers that caress her side. I blink a few times before slowly lifting my eyes, brows raised. Aiden watches me as he kisses the side of her head, claiming her as his own with that simple gesture. I clear my throat. This could complicate my plans. Having lovers in a rebellion is a weakness.

"How?" I ask, my tone clipped.

"How what?" Eliza asks, confusion scrunching her forehead, displaying her innocence and naiveté.

Her head swivels to Aiden when I don't answer.

He shrugs. "It just happened."

I glare, foreseeing this to be quite the issue and all the possible complications this could have. Not only are they risking themselves, but they're risking our cause, all in the name of love in the afterlife.

"Come," I demand, turning on my heel and starting through the forest. Reaper's Breath roams through the trees, a blanket of churning curls, but never straying far.

My head swivels this way and that, keeping a constant watch for reapers delivering shades to their final resting place. I want to snort at that thought.

Escorting souls back to this realm is supposed to be a reaper's job, but Reaper's Breath has intervened every time we ask. Could it be that it's equally tired of Kheelan's games? His unjust punishments? I'll never know, but I believe its loyalties are in the right place. The Death Realm isn't supposed to be like this. The shades shouldn't be his servants, his pawns in his sick and twisted game of entertainment. Death is meant to be peaceful. I think Reaper's Breath knows that.

"Where are we?" Eliza asks behind me.

"The Tween," Aiden and I say together.

I tune him out as he explains everything he's learned during his short time in the Tween while keeping a constant watch on the forest's activities. All seems silent, but I know better than to believe it.

When he's finished, I add, "The Death Realm's entrance is just ahead."

"Dyson . . . where's my mom?" Aiden asks.

I stop in my tracks and turn to face him. "I sent them back." When steel replaces his love-struck puppy eyes, I add, "You'll see them shortly."

"Them?" Eliza asks.

Aiden glances at her. "My mom . . . and yours."

Her breath hitches, her hand flying to her chest. "She's here?"

"Yes," I say. "I'll let her explain everything when we get there."

Swiveling her head to me, she bites the inside of her lip, watching me. I know that look. She's considering how much trust to place in me. Maybe I misjudged her and her naivety.

After a moment of consideration, she squints, turning her head to the side, and takes in the silent forest. "It's so quiet here," she mumbles, breaking her hand holding and rubbing her arms.

I know she doesn't feel chilly—she can't—but the eerie stillness tends to have that effect.

Aiden and I watch her take in our surroundings. She's so innocent. She has no idea what she'll be walking into. Neither of them do. This isn't dream-worthy. This isn't happily-ever-after. This is the closest place to the hell you can get.

"You need to prepare yourselves," I begin. Their eyes return to mine, Aiden's eyebrows pinching together, creating two lines above the bridge of his nose. "What you'll witness . . . you need to be prepared."

Before they can answer, I turn back around and begin walking. I glance back at them a few times to make sure they're still following.

As shades, we don't make a sound as we move. I'm still getting used to that. Even though Kheelan locked my wolf inside me, I still have his extra senses, but they're of no use when it comes to the transparent.

We're getting close; the few score-marked trees signal my direction. I lift my head, watching Reaper's Breath swirl and shape, happily trailing along. What it would be like to be so free. To know no harm can come to me, to be many places at once, providing help while fooling the cruel.

"What's that?" Aiden asks.

Glancing back in front of me, I watch the wall of swirling thick fog. So thick it's impossible to see through. It's the

Reaper's Breath entrance to the Death Realm. "That's our door," I answer.

Once we reach it, I stop, hesitating and coming to a decision. They stand beside me, Aiden on my left and Eliza on his left.

"I want you to stay here. Stay here and stay out of sight until I come back for you," I whisper.

Aiden angles himself toward me while Eliza leans forward, poking a finger into the fog.

"Why?" Aiden asks, his voice equally as quiet as mine.

I stand still as a statue, a feeling of dread overcoming me though I don't know why. "Shades . . . we aren't supposed to be gathering the dead. That's the reapers' job." I look at him. "I need to make sure it's safe."

He shifts his weight. "What exactly are we walking into, Dyson?"

I look back at the entrance, Reaper's Breath swirling, swaying, billowing. It calls to me like it does to every shade. "The beginning of a rebellion," I supply him. "Hide—wait here. Do not enter without me. Wait until I come back, okay?"

In my peripheral vision, I watch as Aiden nods once. He takes Eliza's hand and leads her away, stepping behind a nearby tree.

Taking a deep breath, I walk forward into the thick wall of fog. It covers me, surrounding every edge and dip of my body while pulling and tugging, taking me to my destination.

As soon as I land, I instantly search the area. The entrance to the city of Death is just ahead, its stone arches beckoning me with such a force that it's hard to deny. It's Kheelan's magic, the work of the Fee, to have the strength to build such a call.

The arch has such intricate details that I often wonder if the cruel man has some sort of calling for architecture.

Did it take him years to form the grooves? To design such dread in the form of stone? Or did it come to him on the spot? My guess is the latter. The cruelest of men can have such vivid imaginations.

Beyond the arch is a white brick wall, a path to the inside. The bricks are sporadically placed, like symmetry was a distant thought when this was built. Or maybe it was placed that way on purpose, conveying the disorder and chaos inside.

The city is built of stone, white and gray in color, just like the stone underneath my feet. No natural light exists here, only torched flames that never run out of fuel light my vision. No trees, no animals, no sky. It is nothing like I had envisioned the afterlife to be.

Jane and Tanya hover against the stone wall, their faces lighting with delight before they frown and take a step forward.

"What's wrong, dear?" Jane asks. "Did something happen?"

"Nothing," I whisper, using my hand to gesture for her to keep quiet.

Kheelan doesn't create life, maybe by choice or because he likes to be surrounded by those significantly weaker than he is. Either way, each creation holds a purpose, and his personal army of vampires are no different. They are the ones who guard the city, who instill fear and punishment into each shade. Rumor has it that he built them to search for his long-lost daughter a few hundred years ago. There are many in the Earth Realm, but I imagine they're kept there for a reason. If he or his vampires haven't found her yet, I don't think they ever will. If she's still alive, someone has hidden her well.

"Ready?" I ask Jane and Tanya.

They nod, grins taking over their features. They stand before me, and we walk back into the thick layer together, transporting us back to the Tween.

"Mom?" is the first thing I hear when we exit. Eliza runs forward, leaving Aiden behind to leisurely follow. He stands next to his mother while Eliza throws her arms around Jane's neck. She stumbles back from the force of it and laughs with delight, returning the embrace. A smile stretches over my teeth, a small victory inside a great risk.

I let them hold each other for a moment longer. Tears of happy delight stream down their cheeks.

Eliza looks over at Tanya and Aiden, a look of wonder on her face. "Tanya . . . you- your—I know you."

A little annoyed that they have a loving family reunion that I'll never get, I clear my throat. They can have this conversation later.

"Come on." The four of them glance at me. "We need to get going before we're discovered."

Eliza unfolds her hands and takes hold of Aiden's. She leans into him, and he tilts her chin, softly kissing her lips. A tender love, one that's just blossoming. This is no place for love. I pity them, yet envy seems to drown me.

I turn, gesturing for them to go through. The fog billows, waves, and tendrils like fingers curl toward us, begging our entrance and calling upon everything that we are.

Jane and Tanya nod to one another before they step through. Aiden and Eliza follow one step behind. I wait, taking a moment to gather myself. Hope desperately tries to grab hold. My plan may just work. Their love may not be all for naught, if we're successful. Maybe then I'll be able to find some sort of peace.

Glancing around, I make sure I'm truly alone before I, too, follow. The familiar sensation takes hold, the fog licking every inch of me, heaving and towing. Noise reaches my ears before I can see where it comes from. A struggle, a scream.

The fog clears in a rapid, swift motion, as if it wishes for me to see what's happening as quickly as possible.

Vampires. The white-skinned, black-veined, red-eyed creatures of the dead swarm like provoked wasps. Some have Aiden and Eliza pinned to a wall while others hold Jane and Tanya to the stone ground.

Eliza cries, begging and pleading for the vampire to release her mother. Aiden struggles in their grasps, but it's no use. The vampire slams his back into the edge of the archway stone. Vampires are notoriously strong. His attempts to fight back are futile.

"Stop!" I shout, holding out my hands and rushing forward before I'm tackled to the ground next to Jane.

A vampire hisses, the smell of death splashing across my face with showers of spittle. His red eyes are the same color as the blood he drinks. "Having yourself a little adventure, shade?" he asks me, his lips struggling to form words around his fangs.

I squirm, attempting to loosen my arms, but it's of no use. The weight of too many vampires presses me into the stone, holding me hostage with no upper hand to gain.

Strong fingers grip my arms, lifting me and placing me on my feet. "Take them to the Keep," one of them says, the words a slurred, raspy hiss.

The horde of vampires surrounds us, pushing into the stone archway entrance to the city. A march of sorts to the dwelling of the acting devil himself.

Eliza whimpers, tears streaming down her face as she turns to me. "What's going on?"

"Kheelan. They're taking us to Kheelan," I growl.

"Who's Kheelan?" she asks, wiping away the moisture with the palm of her hand. Aiden attempts to pull her to his side, but a vampire marching behind us hisses, and he drops his hand back to his side.

I continue, "The Fee—the ruler of the Death Realm."

I look away from her questioning eyes. I'm less worried about her curiosity than what fate lies ahead. Shades aren't allowed to leave the Death Realm. I imagine this encounter won't end with a cup of tea and a discussion about the non-existent weather.

CHAPTER EIGHTEEN

KATRIANE DUPONT

MYLA'S PAST

Staggering men pour out of the tavern, surrounding me. I glance around, Corbin nowhere in sight. I shake my head, trying to clear my hatred that causes my eyes to glow, but it's too late. The men coming to investigate have seen them, their faces and bodies frozen in fear for a brief moment.

Two men step forward, grabbing my upper arms with such strength that I wince in pain.

"Wait! You don't understand!" I shout at them, attempting to raise my voice above theirs. They don't listen, intent on a new destination as they march, half dragging me, to the center circle of the town. They smell of sweat and piss, half the men staggering about.

Too quickly, we reach the gallows. My arms struggle in their grasps. "You don't understand!" I yell again as one opens the gate to the cell Myla had been stored in.

Several hands push against my back, and I fall face first inside the cell. They laugh as I struggle with my dress, attempting to stand. I roll over and sit up, fear pricking each nerve across my skin.

A few sneer through the bars. The man who I caught assaulting the woman is the first to speak. "Tomorrow the witch dies."

My eyes widen, and I attempt to stand once more. "No. No, you can't!"

DYSON COLEMAN

DEATH REALM

The same stone bricks pave the path we walk along as the walls tower up until you can no longer see them, giving the impression of no ending and no beginning. Windowless rooms fill the walls, homes for the dead.

Some shades aimlessly roam the path, stopping and staring as we're escorted by Kheelan's vampire army. They press themselves against the wall to allow passage, fear in their eyes. A few I recognize—the few I've managed to recruit. I incline my head, telling them to stand down. Their brows furrow, a silent question in their eyes. I look away, not wanting to draw attention to them.

A vampire shoves me forward, and I stumble, almost falling to my knees. Jane slows, her hand outstretched to help me, when a stick touches her arm.

Electric currents zap her transparent skin, sending waves of visible, blue, zigzagging bolts from one end of her body to the other. She stills, her eyes wide, her teeth clenched. A scream rips from her throat as soon as he releases her.

Aiden, shocked-still at the display of authority until the shriek exits her mouth, goes to her aide. He's halted in his steps when the vampire waves the stick, threatening him with the same fate.

"I wouldn't try it," the vampire snarls.

He glances at me, and I give a simple shake of my head, telling him to obey. We continue our march, even though Jane isn't ready. She hobbles along, urgently trying to gain back her strength.

It's a long walk, never a break in the street's tall walls or the expanse of onlookers. The vampires' feet pitter-patter a threatening trudge against the path. There's never an alley to look down, a tree to admire, a smile to return. Some eyes hold shame, others hold sympathy. I ignore them as best I can, but it's difficult to disregard.

We reach a break; the walls open to a circular clearing. A castle sits on the expanse of stone—The Keep.

It would be an admirable building—walls so smooth they look like marble, towers on each corner, windows lit by candlelight—if it held someone else inside. A better ruler, a better creator, maybe even a better Fee. I can't imagine that all Fee are the same. I have faith that there's one who cherishes those under their care. One with a shred of humanity.

Fear threatens to cripple me, to strike me down and root me to this very spot. Forcing myself to push forward, to ignore it, I search the windows, the unnecessary breath feeling constricted inside my chest.

Large stone doors, matching that of the walls, slide open, the grind causing me to cringe. My wolf growls inside me, startling me.

Black. Pitch-black. I can't see anything.

A vampire lights a match, the strike loud in such a quiet area. He touches the small flame to his torch, and it engulfs it, the fire licking the air, searching for more to feed on. Spreading the fire to other torches, he steps inside, the group wordlessly following.

The room is dimly lit as the vampires continue to light the candles along the wall one by one. Nothing adorns them. No pictures, no décor. Just candles. Aiden stumbles once as he glances at the ceiling. It's hard to tell where it ends—nothing but black dwells up there.

A large expanse with nothing else in it except for the empty stone chair at the far end of The Keep. A small thread of Reaper's Breath slithers along the throne, waiting for its master to arrive.

As I survey all of the archways leading to other areas, a nail scratches against stone. My shoulders hunch, and I grind my teeth, searching for the reason behind the sound.

Dressed in black robes from head to toe, fingertip to fingertip, it's hard to see where his long dark hair ends as it cascades over the cloth. He's a short man. So much so that the bottom of his robe doesn't touch the floor from his chair. In his defense, the thrown is large.

The vampires in front of our group halt. I almost believe them to bow, but they don't. They stand before him like whipped puppies, waiting for their next instructions.

Just as my feet stop, Kheelan opens his mouth, addressing our entourage. "The rebels." His lips turn up with a warm smile, but there's something in his eyes. Something that makes my skin crawl and the hair on the back of my neck stand on end. His voice is much deeper than I imagined it would be, rumbling through the vowels as if they came from such a deep place in his lungs.

"We caught them returning—"the vampire at the front begins. Kheelan holds up a hand, silencing him.

His eyes land on me, and I feel my soul being stripped piece by piece, hope by hope. My sternum bows out against the intrusion—it's as if he knows my every desire, my every wish,

252

exposing it to himself in such a way that I know he knows. It's at this moment, as my mind is being exposed, left bare, that I know he's conscious of what I've been planning.

"I'm fully aware of the situation," Kheelan says after a moment, keeping his eyes on me. He tilts his head, speculating, before tilting it the other direction. His eyes flit between Jane and Tanya, Aiden and Eliza, before they settle on the lovers' intertwined fingers.

Eliza trembles, her body violently shaking as she stands in front of me. Aiden tries to comfort her, rubbing his fingers against hers as he keeps his back straight, displaying as much confidence as he can.

Slowly, at such a leisurely pace it frightens me to my transparent core, his eyes return to mine, hard edges of steel around the rims. "Dyson," he purrs, "you've been a busy little shade." His voice is full of glee, but it doesn't match his stiff posture, his murderous expression. "Gathering troops for a rebellion to overthrow your king? Before we properly became friends? I'm hurt."

He stands from his throne, takes the three necessary steps down to the main platform that we stand on, and walks to our group. His movement is fluid, graceful, putting any feline to shame. He stands before Aiden, two feet shorter and most certainly not as wide, and searches him the same way he did me. Aiden remains unmoved, at least from what I can tell standing behind him. A smile, like the curve of an old-fashioned mustache, lifts Kheelan's cheekbones when he's finished.

Stepping to Eliza, he clucks his tongue before revealing a hand within his long robe's sleeve and lifts her chin, forcing her to look him in the eyes. "Such a frightened little dove," Kheelan coos. Her shaking accelerates, so much so that I fear her knees will give out at any moment, and then he releases her. He takes a step back, his gaze on me, satisfied with all he's learned.

Kheelan claps his hands together. "Let's play a game, shall we?" My eyes narrow as the vampires rustle, their feet restless as they shuffle in their upright positions.

"It's one of my favorites." Kheelan spins on his heel and returns to his throne. "Dyson, step forward."

Frowning, I hesitate, glancing around at the vampires, catching a few of their red eyes. One shoves me from behind, and I stumble forward, walking the rest of the distance. The vampires in front part for me, hissing as I pass.

Slow, agonizing steps, I try desperately to keep the fear from my face, but my fingers twitch and tremble of their own accord.

MYLA'S PAST

I sit in a corner of my cell, frantically working on how I can get out of here without detection. Its then I realize why Myla never attempted escape. She was saving the grace of future witches—of her daughters. I mean, I knew why she did it, but I didn't feel the 'why' until now.

If we have any hope of survival in the future, of our race, the humans must be shown we aren't a threat. We must show them compassion. What it must have taken her to come to the conclusion of her own death—to be so accepting of it. Myla was far braver, far more self-sacrificing than I originally thought.

In order to display our innocence, we must remain so. If I were to leave this cell, if I were to break free, that would only give them something to fear. Myla's daughters, my great, great so on and so forth grandmothers, would be forever persecuted. The witch trials would never end. Escaping would alter history on such a level that my coven—even myself—would never exist.

Accepting my fate, my head drops. I am to die, and there's nothing I can do about it. No one will come to my rescue.

EPILOGUE

DYSON COLEMAN

DEATH REALM

Kheelan watches me as I stand too stiff, too still, before he finally speaks. "It's a little game I like to call Pick a Foe. You," he says as he points at me, "will have to choose. Him," his finger moves as he continues, "or her."

I shift my body, glancing behind me, and know exactly who he has picked based on their wide-eyed expressions. Aiden and Eliza glance at each other before I turn back to Kheelan.

"Neither is a foe," I mumble, my eyebrows pinched.

He laughs, the sound so slick with evil it travels from my ears to my toes. "It wouldn't be any fun if they weren't your friends, Dyson." The smile leaves his face. "You don't play games with your enemies."

At that last sentence, I know his deeper meaning, his double meaning. He's punishing me for betraying him, the man I see as the enemy, and making me kill a friend instead. My carefully planned death for Kheelan now their burden to bear.

"No," I growl, my eyes flashing wolf. My wolf snarls inside me, furious with this man for containing him.

"This isn't negotiable. You will kill one or the other."

Reaper's Breath rests on the armrest of the throne, completely still and unlike the swirling fog I know. It grieves, desperately trying not to draw attention to itself.

"You can't kill a shade," Jane yells behind me. "We're already dead." I hear a scuffle, but I know better than to take my eyes off the fee in front of me.

"Excellent point, Jane," Kheelan says after the commotion ceases. "Let's remedy that, shall we?"

He lifts a hand off the armrest and twirls his wrist, his fingers following in a fan motion. I frown before such a pain starts at the beginning of my toes, the agonizing discomfort of a thousand needles pin-pricking their way through them to my ankles, to my calves. I scream in pain, and it's echoed behind me by Aiden and Eliza. I realize then that he's doing the same to them.

The pain becomes so intense, so strong, that I can't think straight, not even to ask myself what's happening. I want it to stop. I want it to retreat to my toes. Defiantly, it travels to my torso, licking every piece of my insides. I squeeze my eyes shut, gritting my teeth, but it's so intense that I can't hold back my vocal cords from shouting.

It reaches my shoulders, traveling to my fingertips, to my neck. I bow backward, a thousand needles making their way down my spine. *Someone kill me. Someone make it stop.* My wolf howls inside me, not feeling the pain but in great distress.

White hot throbbing begins in my temples, and my face muscles contort. My hands fly to the sides of my head. It grows and builds to an agonizing level, and I scream once more, the sound almost foreign to my ears.

And then it stops. All of it. My body leans forward, my eyes still shut, my hands and knees on the ground. I don't even remember falling to them. I breathe heavily, the sound the only thing I hear until a thud nudges my ribcage. My eyes fly open, my fingers the first thing I see. I scrape my nails against the stone, blinking several times to make sure this isn't a hallucination. I can't see the stone beneath them. My skin is a pale pink, just like . . . just like when I was alive.

My heart thuds again, and again, until it picks a rhythm that best suits it. Pressure in my neck thumps to each beat, and my fingers reach to it, feeling the vein pulse with life . . . with blood.

Fingers clap in front of me, a cheerful, deep-toned giggle forcing my attention to it. I lift my head, my eyes landing on the Fee who's practically radiating energy. I stand to my feet, Jane and Tanya gasping behind me.

Turning my back on the Fee, I seek my friends, finding them gathering themselves to their feet—Aiden helping Eliza from the floor. A fine sweat covers both of them, and I realize the dribble down my back is the same thing. I can sweat.

I jump when Kheelan whispers in my ear, not realizing he had even left his seat. "Now, my dear friend. Choose."

Eliza and Aiden face me, the wonder gone from their eyes as they hear his words.

"I won't kill them," I voice.

I hear his teeth grind in my ear during his pause of response. "If you don't, I will kill them both." He pauses again. "Do you know what happens to someone after they die a second time?" I don't respond, not wanting to know the answer. "They cease to exist, little Dyson. There is no realm that holds the twice dead." His lips part, I'm guessing from a smile, as I hear the saliva slide over his teeth. "Now, choose," he whispers.

"I can't," I mumble, my eyes flitting between them. "I wouldn't even know how."

"Oh, sure you do," he coos. "I'll make you a deal." His voice sounds slightly distant as he leans away from my ear, speaking his next words with a louder tone. "I'll free your wolf. You can use him to play our little game." He sounds so casual like it's an easy solution.

I turn my head to him, blinking rapidly. He leans forward, and I fight the urge to step back. Lips cold as ice land on the skin of my forehead, placing a soft kiss. The moment he leans away, the firm barrier melts, and I breathe so deep, my lungs painfully fill to their brim. My wolf stretches inside with the extra room now provided to do so.

"Now. Begin," he says, taking a few steps back, his vampires parting to give him space.

"I can't," I whine, tears welling in my eyes as I face my friends once more.

"You can, and you will," he booms behind me, his voice shaking the wall as he runs out of patience. "Or I'll kill them both, put their heads on spikes, and let my vampires feed on their bodies."

"No!" Jane and Tanya say together, fighting against our captors' hold.

My eyes shift from Eliza to Aiden and back again. Eliza sobs, her body shaking like a rabbit cornered by a fox. I look once more at Aiden, time seeming to slow down. His eyes close, and his head inclines the slightest. I watch a slow sigh sag his frame before he opens them once more. Determination replaces the sorrow in his eyes, and he nods once, telling me to pick him. I shake my head, my feet wanting to take a step back. His jaw ticks, and he nods once more.

"Do it!" Kheelan shouts.

Tears spill over my cheeks as I begin to slip out of my pants. Lifting my shirt over my head, some of the cloth takes the wetness with it.

Standing naked in the stone room, I breathe deep but in a quick, rapid pace, close to hyperventilation. "I'm sorry," I mumble to Aiden, watching tears begin to stream down his face.

I let my wolf loose, my bones cracking and reshaping. As the shifting process begins, Jane shouts in the background, begging for me to stop. Aiden grabs Eliza, pulls her close, places his hands in her hair at the nape, and kisses her. A deep, passionate kiss. One so full of sorrow and consuming love that it fills the room, shattering my heart into a million pieces. This is my fault. My doing.

I'm shoved to the back of my mind, such a familiar sensation, but for the first time, I wish I was anybody but a shifter. My wolf is being used as a weapon for a sick and twisted game of revenge, of punishment. How am I supposed to live with myself after this? Maybe that's the point.

My wolf whines as I retreat further back inside him, forcing him to take all of it, to feel all of what he's told he must do.

Aiden separates from Eliza, breaking the kiss and resting his forehead against hers before moving her back. The sea of vampires swarm her, grabbing hold of her upper arms as she begs with Aiden and pleads with my wolf.

Shifting his body toward me, he nods, his hands balling into tight fists, his knuckles white. My wolf whines, hesitating his actions while he paces. A shock jolts through his body, delivered by the Fee on the throne, the king of death. My wolf yelps, jumping in his place. Again and again, the jolts deliver their pain-jarring bolts every time my wolf hesitates in playing Kheelan's game. And each time, my wolf grows increasingly restless, wanting to do anything for the pain to stop like any animal would. His thoughts become ragged, desperate, and his actions become less forced and more frantic.

His muscles bunch, his back claws scrape the concrete, and he lunges into the air. Aiden stands still as a statue, brave to the end. Inch by inch, my wolf soars closer, opening his jaws at the last moment and snapping them around Aiden's neck.

Teeth sink through flesh, the tips meeting and clinking together while blood coats my wolf's tongue. Screams erupt in the small room, some with glee, some with sorrow. My wolf fills with regret and yanks his head to the side, ripping out Aiden's throat. He drops to the floor, his paws skidding against the surface with flesh clung to his teeth.

I watch as Aiden clutches his neck, fresh blood gushing between his fingers. He drops to his knees, his eyes staring straight at me through my wolf's eyes before falling the rest of the way. His body goes still, his hand falling from his neck, the life leaving his body. Blank eyes look to the side where his mother is, holding her hand over her mouth, tears spilling for the son she only just met.

My wolf shakes, his muscles and bones quivering as a metaphorical fire builds in the pit of his stomach. It reaches me, even as I watch from inside. He spins on the thick pads of his paws, his mind set on destroying the one who ordered the wrongful death. Keelan's face holds such delight, like a child on

Christmas morning. My wolf's nails scrape against the stone as he barrels toward him, only to be stopped by a row of vampires plowing into his side. He snarls, the fire continuing its build, while held underneath the vampires.

"Enough!" Kheelan demands, his voice rising above all the chaos and bouncing off the walls. The room silences except for my wolf's growls and the cries of loss.

My wolf yelps as bones crack and reshape to Kheelan's will, forcing the shift and bringing me back to the surface. My naked back chills against the stone. I continue my wolf's fight, struggling under the vampires before they crawl off me. They grab hold of my fist wielding arms, lifting me to my feet and facing me toward Kheelan.

"Lessons must be learned," he says as I glare at him. "Unfortunately, I don't think you've learned enough." His face, eyes, and voice address the room. "Lock Jane and Tanya in a black cell."

"No!" Jane yells behind me, her voice a demand.

Kheelan continues though I see him stiffen, "Sentence them to twenty years. Be sure to separate them."

I struggle in the grips of clawed hands, my eyes wide, my heart determined.

"Dyson," he addresses me, "I hope you enjoy your new life. You'll be spending the rest of it in a cell." The vampires begin to drag me away to my fate, but Kheelan stops them by holding up a hand. "I'm not to the best part yet. Let's let little Dyson stick around to hear it."

His eyes shift to Eliza, a sadistic smile, one of the truest of natures, spreads over his face, lifting his eyes, his cheeks. "Eliza, my sweet lovely young lady. You'll be my little queen." He tilts his smile to me. "She'll be in good hands," he says, sarcasm dripping from every word like raindrops trickling down a gutter.

My eyes grow wide, and I struggle, yanking with all my might to free myself. "No," I demand. "No. Let her go. This is my punishment, not hers."

Kheelan ignores me, his voice rising above mine. "Each breath you take, each beat of the heart I gave you, I want filled with all-consuming sorrow. I want to hear you beg for your life to end all the way from your cell to the inside of my chambers. I take her as my queen so that every thought that crosses your mind is filled with blame, knowing that each time I touch her, speak to her, demand of her, it's your fault and no one else's. That is your true sentence, Dyson Coleman." He waves his hand, dismissing me. "Enjoy."

****

Drip. Drip. Drip.

The sound drives me insane. Where is the water coming from? I suppose Kheelan needs water just as living beings do.

264

Do they refuse to clog the leak? Or are they determined to drive their prisoners mad?

Drip.

I cringe, my body shifting against the stone wall I lean against in my seated position. It's dark in here. Zero light. Zero torches. Freezing. So cold that it seeps through my skin, my bones feeling like ice. I can't keep warm. Nothing keeps me warm. My wolf refuses to believe he exists, angry with himself, with the situation, for what he was forced to do. I don't blame him. If I could retreat to a dark corner and let someone else take the lead, I would.

Drip.

My teeth grind as my hands rub my naked body for warmth. "If this is their idea of torture, it's working," I croak to my neighbor. How long has it been since I was allowed water? Food? My stomach grumbles at the thought.

My neighbor babbles before spitting out words. "Mad." He giggles. "Mad, mad, mad."

I glance in his direction though I can't see him. It's an all-consuming dark, so black it swallows me, but at the same time feels hollow, empty. Even my shifter vision can't penetrate it.

I wonder how long my neighbor has been prisoner here. When the vampires come in, holding torches in their gnarled fists, lighting the cells, I catch glimpses of him. His hair is long, his skin dirty, and he looks as though he's from another time.

When I ask his name, he repeats one word: "Gan." He repeats it, over and over for hours, until his voice falls silent.

"Gan," I say, interrupting his fit of giggles, speaking to him as if he were a child. "Let's try again. Okay?"

"Gan. Gan, Gan, Gan," he babbles.

Taking a deep breath, I exhale, fighting off my misdirected frustration before it rolls off my tongue. "Gan. Try again," I say, teeth clenched.

I've been working with him over the past few hours, trying to get him to haunt the Earth Realm, to find Kat.

His voice raises in pitch. "Again. Gan. Gan."

I scoot away from the wall until I reach the bars between our cells. "That's right. Again. Close your eyes, Gan. Find her."

He quiets. My heart thuds in my chest, the blood coursing through my body, thick with anxiety. Kat is my only hope. I'll die down here and not from old age. *Come on, you crazy fool.*

Encouraging Gan to cross the realms isn't as easy as it sounds. Something happened to him, something that made him insane. My instructions seem to be falling on deaf ears. If I could just get him to Kat . . . If I could get him to Kat and beg for help, maybe, just maybe, she'll provide it. That's if she can understand him. I don't know how, but it's better than accepting my fate of certain death.

Finally, he breaks the silence with a hysterical giggle. "Pretty! Pretty, pretty beast."

Frowning, I place my hands on the cold bars and lean my face against its surface, desperately trying to peer in the dark. "Did you find her, Gan? Did you do it? Did you find Kat?"

He doesn't respond, my breath the only thing I hear.

Drip. Drip. Drip.

The door at the end of the room filled with cells opens, spilling light into the dark.

BOOM.

Gan slams into the bars. Eyes the size of quarters abruptly come into my vision. I scream, trying to scramble back, but he has my shirt inside his grubby, transparent hands. His teeth yellow, his hair scraggly, he screeches in my face. It sounds like that of a tortured animal.

My lungs run out of air, my scream quieting until nothing comes out. His wailing lasts several seconds after mine before he lowers his voice, speaking in quick tongue, "The beasty. A daughter of life and death. Two in one. Destruction. Chaos. She will be the end and the beginning." He frowns. "End-inning."

He cackles and releases my shirt before trailing back into the dark, pausing only to repeat the genius of his last words between his loud, unnerving laugh.

Breathing loud huffs, I keep my eye on the spot he disappeared from while frozen in place. His words echo in my head, connecting the dots to things I've already stored there. Myths. Legends. Truths and facts.

I shuffle back a little. "Gan," I whisper when his giggles quiet to a soft chuckle. "Gan. Did you make contact?"

He bursts into laughter again, the sound echoing off the walls, slamming into my sensitive eardrums and obliterating me with hopelessness.

"Gandalf!" a vampire shouts in warning, approaching our cells. "Enough!"

ALSO BY D. FISCHER

| THE CLOVEN PACK SERIES |

| RISE OF THE REALMS SERIES |

| NIGHT OF TERROR SERIES |

| OTHER |

Grim Fairytales Collection

Christmas Stranger

ABOUT THE AUTHOR

Award-winning author, D. Fischer, is a mother of two very busy boys, a wife to a wonderful and supportive husband, and an owner of two dogs. Together, they live in Orange City, Iowa. When D. Fischer isn't chasing after her children or creating worlds while sipping coffee, she spends her down time reading until way past her bedtime.

Known for the darker side of imagination, she enjoys freeing her creativity through worlds that don't exist, no matter how much we wish they did.

Follow D. Fischer on Twitter, Facebook, Goodreads, Pinterest, and Instagram.

DFISCHERAUTHOR.COM

Made in the USA
Monee, IL
24 February 2024